J. SARGEA

"Criminal Justice"

J. SARGEANT REYNOLDS C.C.

"Criminal Justice"

F. Douglas McCord Jr.

Copyright © 2011 by F. Douglas McCord Jr.

ISBN: Softcover   978-1-4568-9302-6
          Ebook   978-1-4568-9303-3

All rights reserved. No part of this book may be reproduced or transmitted in any form or by any means, electronic or mechanical, including photocopying, recording, or by any information storage and retrieval system, without permission in writing from the copyright owner.

This is a work of fiction. Names, characters, places and incidents either are the product of the author's imagination or are used fictitiously, and any resemblance to any actual persons, living or dead, events, or locales is entirely coincidental.

This book was printed in the United States of America.

To order additional copies of this book, contact:
Xlibris Corporation
1-888-795-4274
www.Xlibris.com
Orders@Xlibris.com
96184

Prologue

MARCUS MARTINEZ EXITED the elevator on the eleventh floor of the courtsbuilding in Harris County. He walked with crisp determined steps through the crowded corridors, eager to be done with the meeting to which he'd been summonsed. As he again considered how this summons might play out, however, his stride slowed considerably.

As 'assistant' District Attorney for Harris County, Martinez had built himself a reputation as being a hard-nosed player whose methods of practicing law bordered on unscrupulous. That time has long passed. Since then he has moved into the private sector to defend the very criminals he once prosecuted which brought to him no small amount of scorn from his former coworkers. His manner of practicing law shifted, as well, from unscrupulous to nearly criminal.

Martinez knew that the people he once called friends now seen him as a traitor, or a sell out to a lesser cause, forsaking the greater good of the community for the wealth of the wicked. 'That's the naiveté of the under staff's thinking', Martinez thought grimly, 'but what did those people really know anyway?' They could never understand or accept the truth of the underhanded, even corrupt, nature of this courtsbuilding's so-called justice.

Adorned in his expensive custom tailored suit and sporting his even more expensive Rolex, Martinez ignored the disdainful glances from the court's employees who knew him, or knew *of* him. Smiling, he wondered to himself why they couldn't seem to understand that *this* was the reason he went to law school. *This* was why he missed all the college parties to study for exams and worked all those ridiculous jobs to pay for school.

NO! He made those sacrifices so that he could get rich without breaking his back working one of those hot and dangerous jobs that too many people viewed as 'honest' work. Honesty? HA! A working man can work an honest job his entire life and have *dick* to show for it when he retires. While the company that he'd been working for makes millions from breaking the backs of people just like that poor honest bastard.

"I'm gonna get paid" Martinez said to himself time and again, especially when times got hard. "And that just ain't gonna happen workin' an honest job for someone else."

Years of study followed by years of work in the stale fluorescent lighting of the Harris County courtsbuilding left Martinez' Hispanic complexion pale and pasty. He has since remedied that with his move into the private sector of the legal profession. Better pay and less work offered him more time to get out for fun and sun activities as well as a little additional and much needed work in the gym.

Soon he regained his color and had his body sculpted into the form of young girl's dreams. His handsome Hispanic features were countered, however, by the aura of arrogance and the cruelty that was clearly evident in his eyes, which left him wanting in the romance department. Though some women would often mistake that aura for confidence and become attracted to him, they soon realized the truth if the man and left him far behind. Some women went so far as to file restraining orders against him. Martinez knew those women could never understand him as they could never understand the real world. They were lost in their own candy-coated, make believe realm of reality.

Martinez knew the real world all to well, as well as the true nature of justice in this courtsbuilding. He suspected that this summons had much to do with that very topic. The man who ordered the summons, formerly an assistant to Martinez, was now Assistant District Attorney Keith LeGross. This concerned Martinez because he figured LeGross might use knowledge of Martinez' more questionable deals to curve the meeting to his own benefit.

Readying himself for a blackmail attempt, Martinez decided that as long as he made *some* profit then he would agree to almost anything LeGross proposed. In his mind the only thing better than easy money was free money and if a little extra protection from up the ladder came with the deal then all the better.

Taking a left off the main hall, Martinez quickened his steps once again, determined not to let himself get screwed too bad. LeGross was one of the best negotiators and manipulators he'd ever met. Both skills required quite a measure of charisma and his former assistant possessed oceans full!

Arriving at his destination, Martinez entered the reception area of LeGross' office.

"Hello Mr. Martinez." A pleasant voice called as he closed the door.

Behind a large oak desk stood a gorgeous receptionist adorned in business attire which had obviously been tailored to enhance the fullness of her breasts. The young woman's deep blue eyes sharply contrasted with her fiery hair. Her fair, milky white skin remained unblemished by freckles, which was so common among red haired women.

Recognition stirred within Martinez but he couldn't remember where he'd seen the woman before.

"Mr. LeGross is expecting you." She said, smiling. Her melodic voice floated gently from her full lips.

Martinez glanced at the nameplate on the desk. 'Ms. Jennifer Lane' was printed in simple yet elegant letters but the name didn't help him remember. His eyes rose as Ms. Lane leaned forward to pick up her phone, revealing an ample amount of cleavage.

Taking notice that Martinez' stare lingered around her breasts, Ms. Lane smiled as she spoke, "Sir, Mr. Martinez is here to see you . . . Yes sir."

Martinez finally made eye contact with the young receptionist, tearing his eyes away from the entrapping view. Lane's pleasant smile formed into one of suggestion with a hint of lewdness as she leaned forward even more, inviting LeGross' guest to a more magnificent view. Tugging lightly at the collar of her blouse, she widened the spectacle revealing that she hadn't worn a bra.

Martinez didn't even notice Ms. Lane return the phone to its base. He was so entranced by the woman's charms that he unconsciously licked his lips with unchecked desire. Ms. Lane held her pose, stroking the length of her blouse from the collar to the top button and back, slowly.

"This way Mr. Martinez." She said in a throaty suggestive voice as she allowed her eyes to roam over the man's athletic build.

It took a moment for her words to register in Martinez' mind before he finally acknowledged them with a quick nod, again unconsciously licking his lips. He approached the hallway to the left of Ms. Lane's desk, who met him by sliding her arm around his waist and holding up a card for him to see before escorting him down the short hallway.

"I'm off to lunch now," she explained, "but here's my card. You should call me if you need any . . . mmm . . . *assistance?*"

Martinez managed another quick nod and replied lightly, "Thank you Ms. Lane, I will."

His escort placed her card in his pocket as she opened the door for him.

"Mr. Martinez, sir." she announced, entering the office with LeGross' guest in tow.

"Thank you Jenna. You can take lunch now, but I'll see you in court at one." LeGross stated politely.

Jenna nodded receding into the short hallway and quietly shutting the door.

"Jenna?" Martinez asked incredulously as visions of a young stripper rocked his memory. Jenna had been one of the many young women who frequently pleasured him at his favorite and expensive cabaret on the outskirts of downtown Houston.

LeGross smiled broadly, "One and the same Marty. Come have a seat, we've a lot to discuss."

Martinez winced when he heard the old nickname that his former coworkers knew him by, nevertheless he followed LeGross' instructions and took a seat in the chair indicated to him.

"Brandy?" LeGross asked, handing Martinez a three finger pour of the amber liquid with a few cubes of ice.

"Isn't it against policy to consume alcoholic beverages in the courtsbuilding Keith?" Martinez asked, accepting the crystal glass.

LeGross shrugged as he finished pouring himself a glass and put away the bottle. "We're here to *enforce* the law, Marty, nothing more. I consider this a perk which follows the position."

LeGross' smile broadened as he took his seat across from Martinez. His close-cropped strawberry-blonde hair enhanced the sternness in his northern blue eyes. LeGross' lanky body stood just over six feet and his inexpensive dark suit made his pale skin seem almost translucent. Martinez' gaze was caught by LeGross grossly cheap watch, causing him to wonder what the man did with the additional funds that he was surely acquiring under the table.

Martinez stopped his contemplation and focused his thoughts. "What did you want to speak with about Keith?"

LeGross took a long moment before answering. "Marty, we've known each other far too long to beat around the bush. And to be fair, we probably know too much of one another to be completely comfortable."

Martinez wasn't expecting the blunt statement. He'd prepared himself to be bullied into a corner but LeGross' opening had leveled the playing field, putting the two on common ground. Martinez visibly relaxed knowing that there'd be no attempts to manipulate or intimidate him into making a raw deal.

LeGross relaxed as well, kicking his feet upon his desk and leaning back in his chair. It was his forum after all, so he began, "I'm sure you have a strong idea of why I've asked you to meet with me, you've done this very thing more times than I care to remember."

Martinez nodded his agreement. LeGross nodded as well, and then continued, "This is how it works Marty, just to recap, ok?"

Again, Martinez nodded silently in consent.

"You'll make a show of a defense to your indigent clients appointed to you by the courts, then you'll convince them to make a plea bargain for a 'lesser amount of time'." LeGross raised his fingers in quotation marks as he spoke. "In return, I'll make you a more favorable deal on your obviously guilty yet paying clientele. You'll make a profit from both ends and our jobs will be a lot easier. Our book time will be cut to virtually nothing and my career gets a well-deserved boost. Everybody wins . . . well, almost everybody!"

Martinez stared at the man across from him for a long moment then, clearing his throat and leaning forward, he started, "Look Keith, I've been in the game a long time; long before you. I've proposed this same deal to hundreds of others, as you well know, which is why I'm surprised that you'd leave out even the tiniest of details."

LeGross' smile twisted into a wry grin. "Which detail is that Marty? It has been a few years, hasn't it?"

Martinez leaned back into his seat and sighed, "The trial docket, Keith." He stated flatly, "When my fee from the county raises to the trial fee, then I'll give you the heads of the poor. Not before!"

Both men well knew the underbelly of justice in Harris County. Supplied by three separate county jails in downtown Houston that could hold anywhere from four thousand in the smallest to seven thousand in the largest, the county courts had no shortage of possible convictions. The larger percent of men and women prisoners were in fact guilty, but a significant amount of them who were innocent were inevitably smashed under the wheels of that so-called justice. Innocence here was nothing more than a fairytale.

Martinez recognized himself as an instrument of that wheel, but it didn't bother him one bit. Not so long as the easy money kept rolling in and that's exactly what this meeting was about—*easy* money. Why should he care for the unfortunates who feel under the wheel? After all, those same people didn't care for him when he was being bullied in his younger days. To them he was just another dirty little spic, now they were nothing more than fodder used to line his pockets and fatten his bankroll.

Both men also knew that Martinez would accept the offer. It was easy money that took only a minimal amount of time management and a little manipulation . . . or intimidation. Any day he came to the courtsbuilding he could see four or more indigent clients in an hour's time. Martinez had years of practice in manipulation and the application of scare tactics, and he was very good at *persuading* his various clients into signing nearly anything he wanted them to.

Martinez could tell what type of person he was dealing with from the first visit and sense which buttons to push or where to apply pressure. The whole system was nothing more than a game in which *he* was the professional athlete that seldom lost. Law had so very little to do with what went on behind the closed doors of the Harris County courtsbuilding.

Keith rose from his chair. "Of course Marty, so we have a deal?"

LeGross knew how Martinez would respond, the trial docket was no problem . . . expected even. He had several attorneys on his team who sacrificed their indigent clients in order to gain better deals for their more profitable ones *and* they made a little extra bread as an additional reward. LeGross didn't give a damn one way or the other; he was getting convictions from all around.

The sentence didn't matter at all, only the number of convictions. The Grand Jury is so overwhelmed with frivolous charges that they rarely spent more than three to five minutes sorting it all out and approving indictments. As a result, many innocent people would find themselves facing very serious felony charges.

Facts of lesser crimes, such as would be misdemeanors, could easily be jumbled to make an incident appear to be much more serious. It's not uncommon in Harris County for someone who commits a misdemeanor theft to be charged with robbery or burglary. Possession of an illegal drug would escalate into manufacturing and delivery; a much more serious crime. A man would have one too many drinks and give a woman an innocent pat on her butt then find himself serving twenty years for sexual assault.

The accused are guilty until proven innocent, a proclamation usually preceded by a large sum of untraceable bills passed into the hands of the powers of the courts. If a person couldn't afford an attorney, or bail for that matter, that person would get a court appointed attorney much like Marcus 'Marty' Martinez. And if that was the case, then that unfortunate person would undoubtedly be found guilty and sent to prison.

Martinez finally stood as well, reaching out to shake LeGross' hand, "Yeah Keith, we have a deal."

"Excellent," LeGross responded politely, "I'll see you in court counselor."

Martinez showed himself out, considering an early evening with Ms. Jennifer Lane. LeGross on the other hand had much more *alternative* ideas. The thought of Jenna and him together was revolting, but he kept her around as a ruse or a window dress to throw off would be gossipers. It worked well too, soon talk of the new playboy assistant D.A. and his young receptionist rebounded throughout the courtsbuilding.

LeGross waited a few minutes after Martinez left then placed a call on his cell phone which was picked up on the second ring.

A feminine, yet undeniably male, voice answered "Hello?"

"Are you busy tonight?" LeGross asked, knowing the response.

"Keith honey, where have you been? You know I'll clear my night for you and can bet I'm gonna make you pay for neglecting me for so long, you ungrateful, naughty boy."

LeGross smiled broadly, yes, he though to himself, it's going to be a long night.

* * *

Martinez made his way to the courtroom of Judge 'Big Time' Bill Rights and immediately surveyed his first group of victims to be sacrificed to the assistant D.A., Keith LeGross.

The first unlucky soul allegedly committed a robbery in south Houston. Martinez entered into the holding area through a side door in the courtroom. Sitting down at a Plexiglas window he read aloud the name on the file, "Lane Bryant!"

Chapter One

THE BIBLE READS, "The love of money is the root of all evil." However, most people misquote that passage as *money* being the root of all evil. Lane Bryant knew better; he had seen evil many times in the eyes of men, several of those times he had been looking into his own. NO. Money wasn't the root of evil, nor was the *love* of money, but it sure seemed to be the root of all problems, especially marital problems.

Lane and Carol Bryant had been married four years and their union seemed to be a strong one. Carol was a fine woman, beautiful and faithful. The couple married the same year Lane paroled from prison and three handsome boys resulted from their marriage.

Lane worked out of the pipefitter's local in Nederland Texas, a small town between Port Arthur and Beaumont. Most of the work Lane performed was inside the local refineries and he earned an honest income for his family. Then the layoffs began.

The refineries and their contractors began to lay off their employees who had criminal backgrounds. The background checks went back for seven years and as a result, Lane, who just successfully discharged his parole in the previous year, was caught in the layoffs as well. Unfortunately the local unions couldn't protect their members from the discrimination and many workers became unemployed. Gainful employment became scarce for Lane and eventually he was forced to take a handy-man job for a fraction of his former wages. Subsequently the bills began to pile up and with that so did the arguments with Carol.

One afternoon the couple was discussing a small raise Lane had earned, but it wasn't nearly enough to help matters. Carol, who kept Lane's truck during the day, picked him up from work and as Lane drove home the discussion about the raise somehow turned into an intense argument about money . . . or the lack of it.

After several minutes of the argument Lane calmly stated, "I need a beer." A minute later he spotted a crowded corner store on the opposite side of the four-lane road. Carol began complaining something about how they couldn't afford to purchase those types of vices and Lane lost it.

Instead of entering the turning lane and then slowing to cross oncoming traffic, Lane jammed the gas pedal to the floor and bolted recklessly across the busy street. The maneuver knocked Carol against the passenger door and again into the dash when he slammed on the breaks in the store parking lot. Lane skidded to a stop and exited the truck, slamming the door hard; then he stormed into the store, never looking back. Once he paid for a couple of beers, he walked back out to find that Carol, and his truck, were gone.

Rage filled Lane's heart, burning his chest and blurring his vision. Voices rose in volume in his ears, swirling in and out of coherency. The chaos boiled within as he stood trembling at the spot where he had parked. Hardly aware of his actions, Lane opened one of the beers and drained its contents, drowning out the voices that were screaming in his head. Just as he finished he heard a heavily accented voice from behind him.

"You cannot drink beer here!" A foreign clerk demanded in broken English.

Lane ignored the man. Dropping the empty can at his feet, he opened the next one and drained it as well.

"Sir, you do not drink here!" Lane could barely hear above the returning chaos bouncing around his brain.

All at once every voice in Lane's head was silenced and he heard the clerk clearly.

"You leave here! I call police!"

Lane spun to face the man, his features twisted in rage. All the chaotic voices in Lane's head, which had been fighting to be heard above one another, now spoke to Lane as one. Lane's own hate filled voice joined the entourage.

"Get away from, you fuck!" He commanded the immigrant; violently slamming the empty beer can at the clerk's feet.

"Get away from me before I give you reason to call the police . . . and a coroner!"

Lane's sudden aggression sent the bony clerk running back into the store yelling something in a language that he didn't understand.

The scene caused many of the customers at the fuel pumps and those who were crossing the stores lot to stop. Lane glared at everyone in turn, daring someone to say something. Some of the customers looked away, but some continued to eye Lane suspiciously while others laughed at the whole spectacle and gave Lane a 'thumbs up'. After a moment, Lane shook his head and stormed away, beginning his long march home.

* * *

The summer heat in Port Arthur is cruel and brutal. The humidity, however, is far worse with the city being just a few miles from the Gulf of Mexico and seven feet below sea level but Lane didn't notice the weather during his mechanical march along the busy highway.

The idea that Carol might have cooled off by the time he arrived did little to soothe his own anger, which seemed to multiply mile by endless mile. The fact that no one stopped to offer Lane a ride only fueled his hatred of society and the people in it. This in turn kept Lane's stride steady and full of angry energy. The hours of marching down the sun baked highway and other equally hot roads worked several blisters on Lane's feet. Still, he was full of determination and anger even as he entered the apartment complex where his family was forced to live until the money situation improved.

During the entire trek, Lane never once broke his stride. He never stopped to rest or get a drink of water. His focus seemed unnatural and unyielding as he strode past the sidewalk leading up to his home. Never looking in the direction of his apartment, Lane headed straight for his extended cab Silverado.

Lane wasn't about to fight with Carol for his keys but she hadn't locked the doors anyway. Once inside the truck, he began frantically groping under the rear seat.

"Where is it?" A familiar voice sounded in Lane's ears.

Stopping his search, Lane turned to look into the mirror that was mounted to the windshield.

"What do you need it for!" he asked.

The reflected features twisted into an image that Lane hadn't seen in a long time, and had prayed that he never would again.

"I'm gettin' outta here, you ignorant fuck!" the twisted image responded. "If you're gonna be counter productive then you can get the hell out!"

Lane was completely aware of what was happening. He could feel his hand ball into a fist and his muscles contract but all he could was stare at the evil grin of the twisted image staring at him from the mirror. Powerless to stop it, the fist blow landed a ferociously to Lane's temple on the right side of his head. White flashed in his eyes, then . . . nothing.

* * *

Noise . . . a low humming sound . . . it sounds so familiar. Lane knew that steady hum very well but, for some reason, he couldn't place it. A car maybe? No, not a car, a truck! *His* truck! I'm in my truck, Lane thought groggily to himself.

Darkness lifted from behind Lane's eyes bringing him into the gloom of twilight with lights colored red, orange, and bright yellow and white. He didn't need to open his eyes, they'd been open the whole time, they just couldn't see. *He* wouldn't allow them to see, until now. Sitting in the driver's seat, Lane noticed that the steering column had been busted open to bypass the ignition. Slowly his gaze drifted from the steering column to the rearview mirror.

"What do you want?" Lane asked solemnly as his truck sped along the highway. "Why are you here?"

Lane's soft features took on a predatory sharpness in the mirror. His eyes, which would falter at times, were now steady and calculating . . . and cold.

"I'm here because you brought me here, remember?"

Lane's features softened once more, but remained stern.

"No! I never asked you to come! You just showed up, uninvited."

Another facial shift.

"Don't be stupid!" Lane commanded. "I can't create myself. No body has that power. So that leaves *you*" Lane's features twisted up a menacing grin. "And I thank you for it!"

The spiteful edge in Lane's voice slipped away.

"Don't thank me! Just go away!" Lane demanded.

"Ha! Not likely Lane Bryant. *You* brought me here whether you want to admit it or not! Now I'm gonna have some fun, and you . . . you're gonna relax for awhile. If not, well you know cranky I can get. Don't you."

Of course Lane knew firsthand the horror's that this maniac was capable of. Lane knew his strength too! If he didn't find a compromise with this demon then the situation would get way out of control.

"Yeah, sure." Lane mumbled toward the mirror.

"Good boy, Lane. I'm gonna rest now, I suggest you find a nice quiet motel and do the same."

Lane shrugged, "I need some money . . ."

Before Lane could finish his sentence, his gaze was forced toward the back seat of the cab. The seat had been folded up and about thirty cases of beer were stacked neatly on the floorboard. A new set of clothes and some hygiene were laid on top. Lane knew all too well where the new inventory had come from.

As a homeless street kid at the age of fifteen, he joined a local set of kids who taught him how to survive. Lane had been taught so many different hustles that he could earn up to a thousand bucks in just a couple of days, a fortune for a young kid in his situation. Eventually that lifestyle caught up with Lane and landed him in prison at eighteen years old. That was just the first of several trips through the Texas prison system.

These items found in Lane's truck, however, were the fruits of much less serious crimes. During his times on the streets Lane learned about the local department stores security and how it worked. He could walk into any given store and walk out with just about anything he wanted from food to clothes to color TVs.

In time the stores installed magnetic security systems at the exits to prevent those types of thefts. The system worked by attaching small tags to various items, or placing them inside the item's packaging. If the tags were not demagnetized at the registers, then the system would sound an alarm when that item passed through the exits. But it didn't take long for Lane to learn how to beat this system as well.

The easiest boost at any store was beer. Cases of Budweiser, Bud Light and Miller Lite didn't have the tags required to sound the alarm. The laws governing the sale of alcohol at that time were pretty lax allowing Lane, who looked older than he was, to walk out of the store unquestioned. The nearly risk free hustle would bring up to six hundred dollars every few days.

Lane had given all that up, however. Even when times got tough, like now, he refused to relapse into that old lifestyle. Yet here he was, obviously back to his old tricks. Only this wasn't *Lane's* trick! His demon had returned and was every bit as powerful as Lane remembered.

Lane knew that to ignore the maniac's admonitions would provoke another attack. Eventually, as Lane entered into Houston's city limits, he submitted to the cursed being. He then began to believe that he did need some time away from Carol. The couple had been arguing a lot lately and those arguments have been getting worse. Lane didn't handle stress so well and he knew it, so ultimately he decided that a few days wouldn't be so bad. Hell, he thought solemnly, it might even save his marriage.

After five days of peace and quiet, Lane determined it was time for him to return to Port Arthur. He missed his boys terribly and knew he would have a tough time patching things up with Carol. But he was looking forward to seeing her again nonetheless.

Lane paid for his motel room with the money he made from selling the cases of beer to various people at discounted prices. The room and the food he'd been eating the past five days wiped out those funds, leaving him with just ten dollars. Checking out of the room, Lane realized that he missed the complementary breakfast and he was getting hungry, so he drove to the first restaurant he could find.

Spending most of the ten he had left, Lane paid for his Wendy's combo meal and took a seat at one of the three open tables on the patio outside. Each table was shaded by an individual umbrella and Lane was thankful for the shade.

He finished his hamburger greedily and was snacking on the fries when a voice rang out.

"Lane! Lane Bryant? Hey, Lane!"

Lane looked around to see a black man running toward him in a half jog, half-walk motion.

Instinctively Lane jumped to his feet to defend himself, a habit he picked up in prison. The man stopped in his tracks, recognizing Lane's defensiveness.

"It's . . . It's me Lane, Bit E . . . from Jefferson County! Don't you remember your old friends?"

Of course Lane remembered the name, but it had been years since he'd seen this man that he once called his friend.

Earnest Moore, 'Big E", was very light complected for his ethnic heritage due to one of this grandfathers being white and his other grandmother being Cherokee. The two friends had served time together in the Jefferson County Correctional Facility in Beaumont, Texas when Lane was barely eighteen old, and waiting to be sentenced to the Texas Department of Criminal Justice.

Big E had been a mentor of sorts, teaching Lane how to handle himself in tough situations and how to *handle* someone else in tougher situations . . . permanently. Making weapons from various items, utensils and even trash became a hobby for Lane. Each new creation exceeded the previous in creativity and lethal applicability while E's pastime would be to instruct Lane on the most efficient use and disposal of the deadly items.

Still, Lane was unprepared for prison and the other prisoners picked up on it immediately. Being surrounded by the unknown was bad enough, but when one considers all the unwritten laws of prison politics and the deadly impact of those laws, one can easily feel overwhelmed. From his first day Lane felt that he was expected to participate in a never ending series of brutal battles.

After receiving his housing assignment Lane was pointed to the dorm where it was located. With his linen in hand and a sleeping mat tossed over his shoulder, he made his way in that direction. Along the way, he was passed by a line of field workers walking in pairs toward the opposite direction.

Near the end of the line was a large white prisoner who sported several racial oriented tattoos. The two that stood out the most was a bold swastika on the left side of his neck. The tattoo was back dropped by two blocked-styled lighting bolts.

The second Lane recognized as a pecker wood, a man's body with a woodpecker's head. The tattoo was located at the man's bicep and depicted a peckerwood adorned in the robes of a Ku-Klux Klan member. The hood was clenched in the peckerwood's fist and above its head was displayed '100%'.

The white man stepped out of line and right up to Lane, towering over him.

"You better take care of your motha fuckin' business, white boy!" The tone was serious and threatening; Lane wanted to shrink away but held his ground and forced himself to return the prisoners malicious stare.

"Lambert!" A guard called from the front of the line. "Get back in line!"

After a long moment, the prisoner complied, returning to his spot in line.

Lane made it to his cell with no other incidents, made his new home a comfortable as possible and fell asleep, exhausted. Later that day, near dinner time, Lane set out to investigate the dorm's day room area. The building consisted of four identical dorms, although access to the other dorms was restricted to prisoners who weren't housed therein.

Each dorm was fifty to sixty square yards with two tiers that held twenty-one, two-man cells each. The solid cell door had a small six inch by eighteen inch vertical window with thick criss-crossing wire instead of glass. There was one television mounted eight feet high on the walls at opposite sides of the dorm with metal benches bolted to the floor in front of each. Two rows of five.

There were six dayroom tables set throughout which could seat four men each. Near the entrance to the dorm was a small restroom/shower area that held one stainless steel toilet and sink combo and seven stainless steel shower stalls. This was placed near the guard's control picket so that they could see all activity within the dayroom area.

Lane sat in the back bench near one of the TVs after his brief look around and soon another prisoner sat next to him.

"So where you from?" the stranger asked.

Lane turned to look at the guy speaking to him. He was a small guy, about five-six and one hundred-forty pounds, his dark hair and eyes were in extreme contrast to his pale skin. What was even more in contrast was the dark purple bruise surrounding the man's eye. A closer look, through all the swollen flesh, revealed his dark eye encased in bright red. The guy was hit hard by someone . . . or something.

Finally Lane responded, "Port Arthur."

"Yeah? I know where that is. Near Beaumont, right?"

"That's right." Lane looked back to the TV then asked, "What do you want."

The guy's smile revealed a few missing teeth. Someone really worked him over.

"Ok, I'll cut the crap. You gotta take your heart check!"

Lane almost laughed at the guy, but held it back.

"I'm sure you'd want to wait 'till you heal up a bit."

"Not me. And don't press your luck! I was jumped by three vatoes who dropped jack mack cans into their socks and wore me out." He turned his head so Lane could see the large bandage on the back side. "They split my wig wide, but that'll be taken care of soon enough." The guy paused to let Lane soak up the information.

"That's *my* problem, now here's *yours*. The toads want to see what you're about, so do the woods and the vatoes. So you gotta catch house with that nigger over there. He's a newbie too so don't think nothin' about it. Just go in that cell up there," he pointed to the second tier over Lane's shoulder. "and kick his nigger ass!"

Lane looked toward the cell on the second tier.

"Cell eighteen. Go take care of you business and you shouldn't have many more problems while you're here, so long as there ain't no riots."

Lane knew he had no choice, Big E told him this would happen; told him that it was nothing more than a right of passage, but one that could mean the difference between life and death.

"You don't have to win, but you better be sure that people can tell that guy took some licks too!" E's voice rang out from the past.

Lane slowly rose to his feet and started for the stairs that led to the second tier. Before he could walk away, the guy with the black eye grabbed his arm.

"You handle this, show us what you're about, then there's some people who want to meet with you."

Lane nodded then turned to go but was held back again.

"And don't kill the guy P.A., this is just a heart check. Nothin' serious got it."

Again Lane nodded numbly then headed off to face the challenge. It wasn't pretty and when it was over Lane looked much like the guy with the black eye and the split wig . . . but so did his opponent.

Later in the week Lane was congratulated on his successful check and introduced to several members of the strongest white supremist gang on the unit, who referred to themselves as The Brethren. Lane knew more than he cared to know about any gang and this one didn't seem any different. His late uncle had been involved in a similar group after serving fifteen years in prison. That life eventually led to his death and Lane had no intentions of following.

"Those guys are nothing more than parasites!" Lane's uncle said before his death. "They target the younger generation of whites coming into the system and pump their heads full of shit. Most of the shit is true enough but their motivation is all fucked-up!

"They program these youngsters with an abstract idea of 'white pride' and 'brotherhood', recruit them in as 'prospects' and after a while promote them to soldiers'—which I call a crash dummy!

"Most of the so-called 'Aryans' doing this are never going home, but those youngsters are. And when they finally do, they're instructed to meet with other members who're just as fucked in the head but now they're in the world.

"The older members teach this new generation how to cook crystal meth and send them to transport the drugs or guns or anything else they can make money on. The money goes back to the older members and is used to support the guys who're doing life in prison. The same ones that recruited this new generation in the first place, and recruited them for that very reason I should add.

"Sure the youngsters are making money, but you have to ask yourself if chancing life in prison is worth the risk for this facade of 'pride' and 'family'. Do you really think these men who're recruiting those kids give a damn about anything other than themselves?

"I've been in this shit up to my eyes for over ten years and all I've got to show for it is this fucking tattoo that says I'm a member, but who really gives a shit."

Later that a same year someone had shot Lane's uncle in the back with a shotgun and dumped his body in the Neches River. Shortly after that Lane dropped the local band of hoods he'd been running with, vowing to get involved with anything of the sort again. That included these clown and their surprise was obvious then their scare tactics followed, "It's hard to make it solo. The vatoes don't really care; but the toads, they're the ones always crankin' shit up. And they love young white meat . . ."

And on it went for awhile until it finally sank in that Lane wouldn't be intimidated. The last thing he heard about it was a low-key whisper, "Fuck it! Let the niggers have him!"

* * *

The weeks rolled by uneventfully, until one afternoon. The afternoon that changed who Lane was, and the person he would be . . . forever. That afternoon, Lane returned from his work in the fields to find that his lock had been broken off of his locker and his entire commissary, his hygiene and his extra clothes had been stolen. Lane immediately knew the reason for the theft and he knew it was the Nazis who staged it. They wanted to teach him a lesson and this was just the beginning.

Lane stepped near his cell door and peeked into the dayroom. There he was, the Nazi with the bold swastika tattooed on his neck and he was sitting at the table closest to Lane's cell talking with a member of a rival gang which consisted mostly of blacks. Lane watched the two as they talked for a few minutes, laughing and occasionally looking towards Lane's cell.

Just sitting at a table with a black man was *way* out of character for a Nazi, but then Lane witnessed something that was even more out of character. The two stood and shook hands, a sign of peace and in some cases trust. There was no doubt in Lane's mind that it was the black man who broke into Lane's locker. Confirmation followed soon after when the man turned to leave. On the left sleeve of the t-shirt he wore was a design Lane had drawn in ink to mark his property. Not only did the man rob Lane but he was telling everyone that he did.

Big E had grilled Lane continuously about a felon's *idea* of respect. "When somebody tries to take something of yours, it's not about *that* something. It's about respect, just like everything else in the joint. That person is trying to strip you of your respect, self-respect and otherwise, and that respect can mean the difference between life and death.

"Once you lose your respect it's gone, you'll never get it back! You just can't allow that to happen, if you do there'll be a whole new level of problems that you'll have to deal with. Some of those 'problems' will just be poeple taking your shit from you, which is bad enough, but others will beat your ass just for the fun of it. Some will want you to wash their clothes or clean their cells. This is *not* the type of person you want to be because it all ends the same way. Eventually you'll end up somebody's blow-up fuck doll!

"Listen to me good. If you find yourself faced with any type of disrespect, you better deal with it immediately . . . violently . . . publicly. And make it *bloody*! Make an example of the *first* fucker to cross you so that the rest know that you're not the one to be fucked with! If you don't feel that you could kick his ass, for whatever reason, then kill the prick!

"If you bring an equalizer to beat him down and he survives, then you'll be the one with the shank stickin' out of your neck. Someone will know that you did it and word will spread, but that's the point. Just so long as an investigation can't pin *you*, then you're straight.

"The only alternative is to be somebody's bitch! That ain't you Lane. Nobody wants to go home like that, but it happens . . . *if* a person like that makes it home at all."

Lane remembered it all, word for word. And now he knew who took his shit and what he had to do about it.

Pork chops were served for lunch the following day. Sometimes the butcher doesn't extract the bone when he cuts the meat and Lane found himself with a potentially deadly piece of bone nearly three inches long with an 'L' shape at one end. Not bothering to eat his meal, Lane tore the bone from the chop and hurried back to his cell.

When he arrived, his cell mate was out to work as Lane knew he would be, giving him time to work without interruption. Moving quickly he hung his shirt over the vertical window of the cell door and began dismantling a state-issued razor. Inside the shaving razor were two small blades with holes down the length of them.

Once the blades were free, Lane removed some nylon string from the stitch at one end of his sleeping mat. Using the string he fastened one of the blades to the pork chop bone by weaving it through the holes in the blade. This would keep the blade firmly in place so that it wouldn't slide up the length of the bone or come off altogether.

Lane then pocketed a set of latex gloves that he'd swiped from the infirmary for such an occasion and grabbed his commissary spoon which was made of a strong sturdy plastic. He held the second blade in his mouth, placed the shank in his pocket and waited for in and out.

After what seemed like an hour, the announcement came for the field workers to get ready to go back to work. Lane eyed the speaker high in his cell wall as the crackling voice spoke. With the announcement, all of the cell doors were electronically released. Lane left his cell, quickly heading to his mark's housing assignment.

He knew that both men who were assigned to this cell worked the kitchen. One was at work now, but the man who stole Lane's commissary and was walking around with *his* shirt on, worked the breakfast shift. Lane cautiously looked into the quiet cell to find his mark sound asleep. Quietly he slipped into the cell, pushing his hands into the latex gloves.

Once inside, Lane shoved his spoon beneath a hook in the door jam that was designed to catch a closed door and hold it locked in place. This hook receives an electronic signal from the control picket then raises itself to release the door and allow for an in-and-out. Without the spoon in place there would be no way for Lane to escape, sealing his own fate.

Lane slid the door quietly until he heard the hook 'click' into place. With the door secure, he hung the mark's shirt over the door's window and turned his attention to the sleeping thief. Lane had been cautious, but now that caution quickly began to morph into nervousness, then fear.

He began to doubt himself and, not realizing that he was doing so, began to tremble. He had never killed anyone before and all the preparation in the world couldn't ready him for this . . . nor, he thought for a moment, could he follow through with his plan. Lane turned away from his would be victim, intending to leave, but was frozen in place.

Stunned by the onslaught of sermons preached to him by pastor Earnest, Lane's world seem to fade out of the realm of reality. His mentor's words and phrases sounded audibly in his ears, bombarding his myriad of thoughts and mixed emotions. Paralyzed in a world of chaos and confusion Lane could no longer understand the carousel of voices that had risen within. He felt himself begin to sway as the hundreds of thousands of voices rose and fell in his head, vying for the right to be heard. Suddenly, the carousel stopped spinning and all the voices spoke to Lane as one. At first Lane didn't comprehend what he was being said, but then another voice joined the multitude.

The voice spoke calmly but it was full of hatred, "Better *him* than me!"

All memories vanished in that instant, all thoughts silenced and all emotions were cast into a sea of serenity. Only two emotions remained. The two were largely at odds with one another, but somehow they strangely existed together. Of the two, Lane could only understand one.

Confusion was foremost in his mind. He was confused about what he just experienced and where that last voice came from. That confusion mutated rapidly into panic and Lane spun on his heels ready for a fight only to find his mark sound asleep.

Relieved, then confused once more, Lane furrowed his brow. A profound calmness fell over him then he heard that voice speak softly to him again, "Better *him* than me!"

This time Lane knew it was his voice who spoke, but *he* didn't say anything. Confused again, Lane approached a small mirror mounted to the cell wall above the stainless toilet/sink combo. The mirror was also constructed of stainless steel with a high polish, but the reflected image was distorted and blurry.

"Cut the crap!" the mirror's image spat at Lane. "We don't have time for this shit! If you can't handle this then I'll have to show you how it's done.

Something fell over Lane like a veil cast over an unsightly piece of furniture. Control slipped from his grasp as he unwillingly turned and crossed the small eight by ten cell to stand over his sleeping target. He felt a new surge of boldness, and intense power as he looked down upon his prey,

Then Lane 'watched' himself take careful aim and plunge the makeshift weapon deep into the side of his mark's neck. The man's eyes flew open, wide with panic, then he made a motion to grab Lane's hand in an attempt to stop his death. Lane caught a glimpse of the movement and violently jerked the shank, dragging it across the man's throat. The blade held fast to the bone it was tied to, easily slicing through flesh, severing the mark's jugular and most of his esophagus before exiting his neck.

Unable to scream, the man grasped at his throat trying to stem the flow of blood. When he tried to get up, Lane shoved him back down to the mat and watched the dying man's life fade from his eyes until he stopped thrashing and fell limp.

Another announcement cracked through the cell's wall speaker, "Field squad, turn out."

Bursting into motion, Lane rushed to his knees next to the toilet, rinsing the blood from his gloves and weapon. He spit out the extra blade he held in his mouth, using it to slice through the nylon string tied to the shank and allowing that blade to fall into the toilet. Grabbing a nearby roll of toilet paper, he wrapped the bone several times and stuffed it into his sock. He flushed the razors then removed his shirt and dropped it into the toilet. The dead man's blood was evident on the white uniform top so Lane tried to flush it as well, but it wouldn't go down.

Leaving the shirt, Lane ripped off the gloves, shoved them into his back pocket and dressed himself with the shirt hanging over the door's window. He then lifted up on the spoon stuck in the door jam, releasing the door. Careful not to use his hands, Lane exited the cell and shut the door behind him. He hurried across the dayroom area to the restroom, dropping the spoon in the trash. At the dayroom toilet he took a quick leak and dropped the latex gloves in that toilet, holding down the flush button until they went down. He checked himself in the reflection of a nearby window and took another look to make double sure that the gloves didn't resurface then he turned out for work, barely making it out of the dorms door.

A few hours later the body was found and the unit went on lockdown causing the field workers to turn in early. Lane had long since hidden the last piece of evidence buried beneath a cotton plant in the middle of a hundred acre cotton field at the Texas/Oklahoma border.

* * *

Here stood Big E again, after nearly twenty years, in the middle of Houston over a hundred miles away from the town where he and Lane first met.

"You look like shit, E." Lane stated flatly, awakening from his memories of the past that had been stirred by the presence of his large friend.

"Well I've had a rough day." E spoke softly and frowned at Lane's lack of mirth for their reunion. Still frowning, E pushed on, "Look Lane, you still stay in P.A. right?"

Lane stared at his former friend for a short moment, a quizzical look passing across his features. "Why do you ask, E? What's up?"

Big E took the seat next to Lane and sighed, "It's a long story Lane. The short version is that I'm on foot and need to make it to P.A. by tomorrow morning."

"Nothing illegal I hope!"

"Naw Lane, it's not like that." E leaned in a bit, lowering his voice. "Hell, I was just released from the system yesterday, but on my way home I got myself in a minor fix."

The prison system in Texas, upon release on parole, grants the parolee a fifty dollar check and a bus ticket to wherever in the state he/she is being paroled to. Most everyone goes through the Houston Greyhound bus station on their way to their respective destinations. Lane nodded, glancing down the block toward the Greyhound station.

E settled back into his chair, relaxing a little then continued, "Anyway, I met this pretty young yellow-bone, man this girl was fine! Well, it turned she wanted to be with me for awhile, ya know while we were sitting out our layover at the station. Of course I was game; you know from experience what a few years in lock up can do to a man.

"She floated the bill for the room and everything. The trick slipped me a micky then robbed me! She got me for the two hundred I had left from the inmate trust fund and what was left of the money the state released me released me with. The bitch even took my bus ticket. *My fuckin' bus ticket*! I mean if she lives in Houston why would she need the ticket?"

Lane grinned at last, "Since when is Big E, the pimp of P.A., a sucker for any little dirty-leg that bats her eyes his way?"

Not a little agitated, E sharply retorted, "Since the man locks a nigga up for twelve years. That's when!"

Lane laughed openly now and soon E joined in as well. Mack told him "The skank probably was being pimped by the guy who runs the hotel room where she burned you. She'll end up scalping the bus ticket for half its worth just to get a meal and a pack of smokes. Have you been gone so long that you've forgotten the game?"

"Twelve year Lane. Twelve long damn years."

Lane understood completely, "People in this area know that most everyone being released from T.D.C will come through this bus station. Not a bad set up for some small time hustlers!"

"That's great Lane, you just congratulated the cunt that hustled me."

Lane's grin faded, "I remember how hard it was back in Port Arthur, before my first rodeo and if it wasn't for you I probably would never have survived. I haven't had the chance to thank you for lining me out."

Big E spread his hands apart, "Well Lane, here's your change. I was supposed to report today to my Parole Officer but I borrowed a cell phone and called his office, told him I got confused and missed my bus. He understood but told me if I wasn't there by nine a.m. tomorrow, he'd have me sent back to prison by the first of the week. You know the drill Lane; I shouldn't have to go through the details."

"No, no. That's cool. I'm headed that way, bro." Lane said as he got to his feet and slid his uneaten fries toward his friend. "It ain't much to eat E, but knock 'em out, let me grab my refill and we'll cut out, alright."

"Hey thanks, Lane. I owe ya, you're a life saver!"

"No E. I haven't forgotten what you did for me back then. What you taught me probably saved *my* life!"

E smiled and nodded as Lane went to refresh his drink.

* * *

The two had discussed the events which led up to Big E's incarceration and Lane's life and family since his latest release. E was rambling on about how big his youngest had grown and how he'd be trying to patch things up with his ex-wife when Lane mumbled, "aw, shit!" stretching the exclamation out in a long drawl.

E looked at the traffic ahead and at the sides of them on the highway, then at Lane who stared grim faced at the dash in front of him. "What is it Lane? What's wrong?"

"I'm not sure. I'm either low on gas or the gauge went on the blink."

E titled his head, "Please say that we have enough to get home."

Shaking his head Lane replied, "I'd be lying. The truth of it is I don't know how much fuel I have, I just know that according to this," Lane pointed to the fuel gage which was entering the red zone "We don't have enough to make it out of Houston, much less all the way back to P.A. I just spent my last dollar for something to eat. Damn, I don't need this shit!"

"That makes two of us." E echoed. "Let's find a busy store or gas station and I'll try to gather a few dollars from the people there. Someone in this damned city has to have at least a small heart!"

"That's what we're goin' to have to do 'cause I'm not willing to take the risk of being stranded down I-10 in the middle of nowhere. At least in town we'll have a chance to turn over enough cash to get us all the way there. Hell, it shouldn't take more than twenty bucks or so."

Lane exited interstate highway 10 onto a long, nearly deserted feeder lined with abandoned stores that had long been out of business. In the gravel lot of an empty building that had once served as a motel stood a woman stood waiving her hands in the air in an attempt to gain someone's attention. Farther back in the lot sat a light colored SUV with the hood up and white smoke roiling out from the engine.

"Pull in here Lane," E said excitedly, "We can make enough cash here to get us home!"

Lane guided his truck into the abandoned lot, coming to a slow stop near the woman who took a quick look at E then circled around to the driver's side of the truck.

"Typical." Lane heard E state flatly.

"Looks like you could use a little help." Lane said cheerfully to the woman as he set the truck in park and killed the engine.

"Oh please! I don't have a phone and I can't leave my brother's truck here like this!"

"Well, let me take a look at it and see if I can figure the problem." Lane said, descending from his truck and heading toward the distressed vehicle.

"Thank you so much! I don't know what I would have done if *someone* hadn't stopped."

"It's no trouble." Lane responded simply.

After awhile Lane discovered that the SUV ran out of water because the water pump quit working. He also learned the woman's name, Vikki Roberts. He explained the problem and offered to tow the SUV to the nearest station where she could call for a tow truck.

"If you can tow me that far couldn't you tow me just a few more miles to my home? I'd be glad to pay for your help once we got there."

Lane glanced at Big E who winked back to him. "Sure. I can do that, but we'll have to get gas as soon as possible or we'll be stuck all over again."

"That's ok; I've got a gas card. We can fill it up down the road then I'll give you some cash when we get to my home." Vikki gave a relieved smile and Lane thought that she was just the help he was looking for.

Big E helped Lane set up the tow equipment then got behind the wheel of the SUV while Vikki rode with Lane so that she could navigate. The trio filled Lane's truck with fuel and a half hour later was parked on the road in front of the Roberts residence.

When they arrived, Vikki turned to Lane, "If you want to come in for a moment, I need to make a quick call then I can give you a few bucks. I might even have a couple of beers for you and your friend."

A smile crept on to Lane's face, a cold beer sure sounded good! The two met with Big E in the drive way.

"Think you can handle the gear while I collect our earnings, E?" Lane asked as Vikki continued toward the house.

E looked a little irritated but his features quickly turned up a mock smile toward Lane. "Yessa massa! I's thinks I's can manage. Yous goes ahead with littles Miss Whities over theres an' I's takes care o' dis heres, sir."

Lane shook his head as he turned to follow Vikki, "Always a smart ass, E."

When Lane caught up with Vikki in the house, she reminded him that she had to make a call and offered him a beer from the fridge. Lane sat patiently at the dinner table, staring out the window into the back yard and sipped the beer while Vikki talked on the phone. Pieces of her conversation drifted through the house to Lane's ears.

". . . combination . . . give him . . . money . . ."

After a few minutes, Vikki came into the dinning room where Lane waited. She had changed and now wore a light colored men's t-shirt whose material was worn and slightly transparent, revealing Vikki's small firm breast. Her large dark nipples stood erect, pressing against the flimsy fabric of the shirt. Lane took in the view with a mixture of desire and embarrassment.

Vikki's round tan thighs were exposed clear up to her simple white panties where the t-shirt she wore just fell short of preventing the exposure. Lane rose quickly to his feet as Vikki approached with a folded bill in her hand.

"Here you are Lane. Thanks for the help, I really don't know what I would've done if you hadn't stopped."

Lane tried to swallow the lump in his throat. "No problem, Ms. Roberts. You've helped me as much as I've helped you." He managed a smile as he stuffed the hundred in his pocket.

Vikki returned his smile and continued her way to the kitchen, brushing her breast lightly against Lane as she passed. "You and your friend want a few beers for the ride home?" She asked innocently, opening the fridge and looking over her shoulder at Lane.

Lane was able to find his composure once more. "Sure. That'd be good. Thanks."

Vikki pulled six beers from the bottom shelf of the fridge on at a time. Each time she reach down, her shirt rose higher up her back showing her g-string and all her womanly glory. Lane was entrapped and, as much as he knew he should, couldn't look away.

Vikki bagged the six-pack in paper and stepped in close to Lane as she handed it to him. With her hands behind her back and her hair pulled into a ponytail she looked up to Lane. In this posture, Lane could see all the fullness of her breasts.

Barely brushing her dark, erect nipples against Lane she asked in the most seductive voice she could muster, "Wouldn't you want to rest awhile before you drive back to Port Arthur?"

Lane wanted to drop the beer, toss the woman onto the table and have rough, wild sex with her. He envisioned himself tasting her from inside while she pulled his hair. He could hear her cries of pleasure as he entered her with her firm round thighs wrapped tightly around his waist and a plump nipple in his mouth.

"I really need to get home to my wife Ms. Roberts." Lane finally managed with a cough.

In an instant, Vikki's features changed from warm and inviting to cold and selfish.

"Fine!" She spat and turned away. "Be careful Lane." She said with finality as she dropped into a plush chair in the nearby den. Grabbing up a remote control she threw a leg over one arm of the chair exposing her womanhood devoid of all modesty.

Lane watched for a moment as Vikki searched for a channel she liked then threw the remote on the floor. She placed her now free hand between her thighs, rubbing herself a couple of times. Suddenly she stopped, looking at Lane.

"You'd better get going if you want to make it home early." She spoke in an unpleasant tone.

Lane nodded then made his way toward the front of the house. At the front door, however, he couldn't stop himself from looking back. Vikki now sat on the edge of the chair with both of her feet planted firmly on the floor, leaning forward with her elbows on her knees.

She stared straight at Lane, "*Get out!*" she screamed.

Lane exited the brick home but before he could shut the door, the remote control Vikki had used earlier exploded against the door jam near his head.

"Bastard!" He heard Vikki scream from inside.

The sudden change in the woman disturbed Lane, but he didn't want to stay to find out what was going through her mind. He quickly shut the door just as another unknown object exploded against it. Lane made a break for his truck with beer in hand.

Big E had the engine running so that he could wait in the ac, and was unaware of Lane sprinting from the house until Lane opened the driver's door. He was resting his head back on the seat with his eyes closed, listening to the radio when Lane jumped in the cab.

"That's one crazy bitch, E." Lane said excitedly, jamming the truck into drive and peeling away from the curb.

As they sped down the street Lane could see the woman through his rearview mirror standing in the road in her shirt and panties, then she disappeared toward her house.

"What the hell happened?" Big E asked curiously.

Lane ignored the question for a few minutes, navigating the vehicle onto a busy road, through traffic and onto the nearest highway.

"Well?" Big E finally pushed again.

"Well . . . I really don't know." Lane shrugged helplessly, glancing at his friend.

"First she made a call. Then she pays us a hundred bucks and gives us this beer," Lane indicated the brown paper bag, "then she freaks out and starts throwing shit at me, cursing and screaming."

"Why would she do that? The way she was acting earlier, you'd think we saved her life?"

"I don't know, man." Lane said exasperated. "But that bitch ain't right."

After a short pause, Lane finished, "I don't like that shit E. That bitch is crazy! I don't like it at all!"

"Yeah. She don't sound right." Big E pulled a couple of beers from the sac, handing one to Lane. "She don't sound anyway near right!"

* * *

Vikki ran out into the middle of the road in her t-shirt and panties. She knew at least one of her neighbors had seen Lane run from her house with a paper bag under his arm then speed down the road. Still she needed a license number and she nearly got it before the truck was too far away. Two, six, one dash D.

"Vikki? . . . Vikki!" She heard a neighbor call to her, "What happened? Are you ok?"

Vikki turned and ran into her own house to the safe which held fifteen hundred dollars and approximately eighty thousand worth jewelry and rare coins. Quickly she scooped all the items into a small purse and ran off to hide the goods. Shortly after, she ran into the front yard with a cordless phone in her hand "Hello! Police? I was just robbed!"

Chapter Two

HOUSTON PD DETECTIVE Dave Osbourne had been the senior detective in robbery for ten years. In that time he has accumulated more arrests leading to convictions than any of his predecessors of the last fifty years, an impressive career to be sure but not one without controversy. The publicized ceremonies awarding officers whose deeds rose above and beyond that of the call of duty had honored Detective Osbourne on several occasions for his "selflessness and valor in the service of this great city". However, in the darker, far less publicized corners of the Houston Police Dept. Osbourne had been accused of many unorthodox and 'questionable' activities, including accepting bribes and even organized crime. With eight internal investigations, and just as many partners, behind him, Osbourne had convinced himself that he was untouchable.

The investigations had all closed for various and somewhat vague reasons. Some closed for lack of evidence and some because a potential witness wasn't willing to swear a statement or the witness just disappeared. Some were just closed.

Osbourne stood about five feet eight inches with a barrel chest and balding brown hair. His solid build and sharp, quick eyes gave him an air of intimidation despite his height. His dress was starched, dark khakis with a sharp crease and a light colored bottom down dress shirt. Black dress shoes with a high shine, a nice watch and manicured nails hinted at his uncanny attention to detail.

Osbourne's latest partner, Enis Von Eric, followed the example with his simple yet meticulous dress. Yet with his boyish features, a very neatly trimmed haircut and clean shave, Von Eric portrayed the aura of an aristocrat who became a cop simply for the action. The two had been partners for the last thirteen months and had many disagreements regarding proper procedure, excessive force and tampering with evidence. Several of these discussions had turned into heated disputes, one ending abruptly when Osbourne struck Von Eric with a clenched fist in the side of his head. Detective Von Eric secretly assisted in internal affairs latest investigation, but the case followed the ways of the previous investigations. Von Eric had conceded afterward, knowing something was amiss and realizing his powerlessness at that point.

The two had arrived at the station late in the morning and met in one of the offices used to question witnesses, suspects and other persons of interest. "Ms. Roberts should be here soon to look through the photo array and give her sworn statement. Let's be professional and efficient so we get this case closed and move on to bigger fish. Agreed?"

Von Eric, not looking up from the file in his hand, nodded his agreement. He knew he'd just be wasting his breath anyway. He felt like he was trapped between the teeth of a large sprocket placed in the innards of an even larger clock and as the seconds dwindled down he could only wait for the teeth of another sprocket to fill the gap in which he was caught and grind him into oblivion.

The office the two met in was bare except for a small table with a coffee pot, a long hard wood table and a few folding chairs.

There came a knock at the door, "It's open." Osbourne said to the door.

An officer in uniform stuck his head through the opening, "There's a Vikki Roberts here to speak with you detective." he said towards Osbourne.

"Send her in, Kyle, we've been expecting her." Osbourne said with a wave of his hand.

The young woman was rather pretty with long solid black hair, her green eyes in contrast with her light brown skin hinting at a Caucasian Hispanic mix.

"Hello Ms. Roberts!" Osbourne said rising to this feet on the opposite side of the table. "Please, come in and have a seat. This is Detective Von Eric; he's been working this case with me."

Von Eric extended his hand as he approached the witness, "It's good to meet you Ms. Roberts, I'm sure we can get through this morning rather quickly and you can get on with your day." Von Eric flashed a disarming smile but it didn't prevent the obvious tension from showing on Vikki Roberts face.

Von Eric stopped short for a moment, his smile fading.

"You can call me Enis." He said, a slightly concerned look spreading across his boyish features.

Vikki Roberts' shaky voice said, "Thank you Enis. Detective Osbourne." She said nodding to the senior detective and allowing herself to be guided to the hard metal seat in front of Osbourne with that seemed to be a forced smile, clutching her small pink purse close to her. Von Eric sat on the edge of the table a short distance from Roberts' left and began taking account of her movements, expressions and the way she structured her sentences and phrases. What stood out the most aside from her apparent tension, Von Eric thought, was the fear in her voice and the suspicion behind her bright eyes.

"Ok, Ms. Roberts." Osbourne began; all business now. "With some luck and your help this morning, we may be able to issue a warrant for the suspect by this afternoon. Do you have any questions before we start on your affidavit?"

After a short pause Vikki Roberts asked curiously, "What's an affidavit?"

Before Detective Osbourne could speak, Von Eric answered, "An affidavit is a sworn statement that will hold up in court, even in your absence. However, if a case such as this goes to trial the defense has the right to cross-examine you."

Osbourne shot a hard look at Von Eric, but the younger detective plowed ahead. "Your sworn statement needs to identical to your testimony at that time. If it's not, the defense could win the case *and* it would be possible thereafter to file charges against you for filing a false report. So we must be as detailed as possible."

Detective Osbourne quickly jumped in at that point. "But we don't need to worry about a trial. I'm confident that, with this particular suspect, it will never come to that."

Osbourne leaned forward, placing his forearms on the table and locking eyes with Roberts in an icy stare he finished in an even colder tone. "You do understand, don't you Vikki?"

Von Eric, who'd been studying Roberts, watched as the intimidation he'd put on her from his speech transformed into stark terror as Osbourne's words fell into silence. Von Eric could see the murderous intent in his superior's cold eyes and a chill coursed through the junior detective's spine. He decided then that he would put in for a transfer as soon as possible.

Von Eric kept quiet for the rest of the interview, watching Osbourne all but *tell* the witness what to say in her affidavit. It took nearly an hour for Roberts to give as accurate an account as possible, but she never once lifted her eyes from the table. The senior detective recorded her statement, without interruption.

Once she was finished, however, he began to question her. "Just to clarify some parts of your statement, Ms. Roberts, I'd like to go over it again so the courts can have a clearer picture of the events you've just described."

Without waiting for a response, Osbourne pushed ahead. "You've mentioned that you now take prescription drugs to help you sleep at night. Is that correct?"

Without looking up from the table Roberts timidly answered, "Yes sir, but I don't think it has anything to do with this."

"Has you doctor said as much, Ms. Roberts?"

"Well, no. We haven't really discussed what happened in any great detail."

"But you did tell him that you were attacked and since haven't been able to sleep well, correct?"

Roberts began to fiddle with the purse in her lap. "Well yes, but not just the attack. There are . . . other things to consider."

In fact, Osbourne already knew about Roberts' psychological issues as well as her heroin addiction, it's how he met her in the first place. Vikki Roberts was a sex addict, so when Osbourne busted her for heroin she offered to trade sex for her freedom. Osbourne was more than happy to make the deal, then Vikki found out what kind of monster Osbourne truly was.

As the aggressor in their first encounter, Roberts had thought that it was a one time deal. Osbourne, on the other hand, had no intentions of letting the disturbed young woman go so easily. The relations continued with threats of jail . . . and worse. The detective would bring her heroin to get her high then choke and beat her during intercourse. Often she would wake up with swollen eyes and dark purple bruised around her throat from Osbourne's indulgences.

Once, when Osbourne had pumped her full of heroin, he took her anally so rough that she had to be admitted into the emergency room but it didn't stop there. Often the detective would prostitute her, mostly to city and county officials who would treat her just as bad as he . . . sometimes worse. He would then blackmail those officials, but all Roberts got for troubles was a free get out of jail card. Even now as Roberts sat across from the senior detective, he held eight thousand dollars worth of her family's coins and jewelry stowed away with fifteen hundred dollars in addition to the other collections he's made throughout his career.

Hoping that Roberts would keep her drug addiction and nymphomania to herself, Osbourne asked the next question with a frown.

"Is there something else, more prevalent than this crime, that has had as profound an impact in your life at this time?"

For the first time Vikki Roberts looked at Osbourne, then quickly resumed her stare at the table.

"No." Came the simple response.

"Ok. So since the attack you need to take medication to help you sleep. Is that correct?"

"Yes sir." Roberts said timidly.

"It's important that those types of facts are clearly stated for the members of the court who haven't had the pleasure of meeting you." Osbourne continued in a slightly scornful tone.

"Now when the suspect told you that he had a knife, did he show it to you or did you by chance get a glimpse of its size and shape?"

"No sir. He never said he had a knife. I think he said that he had a wife back home. I've said as much in my statement and I didn't see any knife at any time during the encounter." Roberts felt trapped.

Intimidated by the speech about being charged for filing false reports and not wanting to bring the wrath of Detective Osbourne on her, Vikki didn't know what to say. She just made a sworn statement that Lane told her he had a wife, now Osbourne was asking about a knife instead. She looked fearfully at the senior detective.

Osbourne set his pen on the table and leaned back in his chair, folding his hands in his lap and crossing his leg. His piercing glare, shifted from the witness to his partner who watched in unbelief. Von Eric realized that if things went awry regarding this statement, he could be implicated.

Osbourne was practically 'forcing' this woman to make the statements he *wanted* her to make; sworn statements that could undoubtedly land the woman in jail. Filing a false report was a pretty serious offense in Harris County, but then all offenses in Harris County, no matter how minor, had the potential to land some body in prison. That is if the police report and affidavit read a certain way.

That's what Osbourne was doing here, twisting facts to ensure a felony conviction.

"Ms. Roberts why do you suppose this person who robbed you, *and* sexually assaulted you, take the time to explain that he had a wife back home?" Osbourne couldn't hide his smirk when the shock of that statement shot across Von Eric's face.

Confusion was apparent on Robert's face when she looked to Osbourne, "I wasn't sexually assaulted detective." She said innocently.

"Of course you weren't raped, Ms. Roberts, I'm not suggesting that. Anytime someone lays so much as a finger on another without his or her consent, it is considered assault by law, do you understand?"

"I don't mean to sound lewd, Ms. Roberts, but what else could it be called when an unknown man grabs an attractive, defenseless, young woman without her consent?

"And if you say that you consented, or that it didn't bother you that much, a good attorney can get him off the hook possibly by saying that the money he robbed from you was in fact a gift. He may possibly be so bold as to say you *paid* him for sexual favors.

"Is that how you'd like to be viewed by the people handling this case?"

Staring down again with tears in her eyes she shook her head, "No. No, of course not."

"Of course not. We don't want that either. That's why the law has provided us with a very complex language and requires that we be very specific when using that language in our affidavits. To protect victims such as yourself, from the more clever, howbeit less moral, defense attorneys."

Detective Von Eric had enough of the mockery. Standing from his perch at the edge of the table he walked to the coffee pot in the corner and poured himself a cup. He wanted to leave, but procedure required at least two officers to be present during these interviews.

"So now," Osbourne continued, "the main points in your statement are that he told you he had a knife, he grabbed you in a sexual manner and he took an amount of cash adding up to approximately fifteen hundred dollars in addition to approximately eighty thousand dollars worth of jewelry and rare coins. All of which are listed on form One-A-Seven and that you have produced receipts for. Did I miss anything Ms. Roberts?"

Vikki Roberts shook her head weakly.

"Very good! Now if you'll just have a look at these photos and identify which suspect it was that committed these offenses."

Roberts indicated the photo of Lane Bryant and Osbourne noted the identification in her affidavit.

"Ok, just sign here and we'll be done."

Roberts signed the affidavit and Osbourne, handing the paperwork to Von Eric, said "Go and get Ms. Roberts a copy of this for her to give to her insurance company."

To Vikki he said cheerily, "Hopefully you can recover most of the damages from your insurance."

Von Eric left the door open behind him when he exited the room. Detective Osbourne reached across the table lifting Vikki's chin so he could see her teary eyes, "You did real good Vikki; I'll be in touch with you soon."

Then he released her and withdrew a card from his wallet, jotting a number down on the back as he spoke, "This is my card; I want you to keep it just in case. On the back is a phone number to an organization for victims of violent crimes. I want you to contact them and describe your case; they may want you to fax the paperwork Detective Von Eric is getting for you now. They have been known to help victims similar to you with finances for various things such as doctors, rent, food and counseling. I'd advise you to take advantage of their services Ms. Roberts."

Osbourne smiled a disarming smile, gathered his paperwork together and rose to his feet as Von Eric returned to the room.

"Well, Ms. Roberts, I believe we have you all fixed up. We'll be in touch to keep you informed of our progress and court dates, in case you'd want to see the proceedings. Just be ready in case you need to appear at the trial, but I highly doubt that it will come to that."

Osbourne crossed the room and called out the door for Officer Kyle to escort Vikki Roberts to her car. After Roberts' departure Osbourne shut the door and turned to Von Eric, "Ok, Enis, I know it's eating you up so spit it out."

Von Eric couldn't imagine where to begin so he just stood there, mouth agape. Osbourne stared at Von Eric for a long moment then nodded and crossed the room to grab the file and his belongings.

"This is a cloudy job, sometimes we're forced to draw conclusions from the small amount of info we can get."

Finally Von Eric found his tongue. "You forced that statement from her Dave! You told her what to say whether she wanted to or not. Why would you do that?"

"Bryant is guilty whether you like it or not. I just made it easier for the courts to convict him, that's all!"

"The guilt or innocence of Bryant is for the court to decide not Dave Osbourne. If that witness caves during further questioning we could be implicated in a conspiracy to frame the suspect."

"Relax Enis! It'll never come to that, Bryant has a history of convictions ranging from burglary to man slaughter; he won't risk taking this case to trial, if he's smart, and if the case won't go to trial there's no reason for the witness to be questioned any further."

"Now, there's an opening in homicide. Maybe you'd be more content working an area that doesn't have as many . . . grey areas to work around.

Von Eric glared at Osbourne for a long moment, "I was just thinking that very thing Dave!" he snapped, then he left the room leaving the door open behind him.

After Bryant returned from his trek to Houston for his vacation of sorts, he and his wife Carol had a tremendous fight which had nearly led to a separation. In the follow week the couple had managed to work things out, but the biggest help to them was when Bryant landed a job working as a deckhand on a tugboat for a local tug boat company. The pay was ok but Bryant had to stay on the boat for three weeks his first hitch then he'd have a week off. Thereafter his normal hitch would be two weeks on the boat and one week off. That eased the tension between him and Carol a great deal and when he returned home for his week off, the two lived like newly weds all over again.

During Bryant's first hitch, Carol received a call from an officer of the Port Arthur crime lab and was asked if they could come take photos of Bryant's Chevy. After she heard their explanation for such a request, Carol, not knowing how to respond, agreed

"There was a robbery Mrs. Bryant and the witness was able to get a partial license plate number. One of the vehicles it matched is yours but there are other matches of course. This is just procedure so the witness can get a visual of all possibilities and, with luck, give us a positive I.D."

The following day, the lab officers had arrived at the Bryant's apartment, performed their respective tasks quickly and efficiently then was gone. Carol had discussed it with Lane when he had his first week off, but the two hadn't heard any thing else about it since, so naturally it was forgotten.

The following October was warm and humid which was the norm for that part of the state. Carol left the couple's three boys with Lane's mother, Mary, while she went to pick Lane up at the docks. Mary happily watched the boys play in the grass outside the Bryant's apartment. Her joyful expression faded into one of scorn and distrust when two patrol cars pulled into empty parking spaces directly in front of her son's home.

An officer exited from the driver's seat of each unit and walked up the sidewalk. The boys stopped what they were doing as the oldest of the three yelled at the cop.

"You'll never take me alive copper!" He proclaimed as he began shooting the officer with his finger.

His younger brother followed his lead, "Yeah!"

The youngest of the three wouldn't be left out of the fun, "Ca'-er!" It was his best attempt at copying his elder brothers.

Smiling at the kids, the officers ask Mary, "Is this the Bryant residence?"

"Yes." Mary answered, not trying to hide the look of disgust on her face.

"We're looking for Mr. Lane Bryant. Is he home?"

Rising from her seat, Mary stepped to the nearest officer, "Well that depends on whether or not you have a warrant." She spit the words out spitefully.

"Yes ma'am," The officer responded politely, "we do have that. Is he home?"

As the exchange continued, the second officer slipped quietly toward the sliding glass door at the patio trying to get a view of the apartment's den.

Mary suddenly spun around, breaking off her conversation.

"You have yet to produce a warrant for my inspection, sir." She said, her tone full of venom. "I suggest you remove yourself from that door until you do or I'll be forced to file a complaint for invasion of privacy or illegal search and procedure." She smiled cruelly, "I might even push a complaint for unlawful entry."

The stunned officer raised his hands defensively, a wry grin spread across his face.

"Would it be alright if we looked around?" the first officer asked, knowing what the answer would be.

Spinning back around to face him, Mary very rudely stated, "*No* that would *not* be alright. He's not here at the moment and I still haven't seen any warrant. If you intend to wait for him then you'll have to do it someplace else, you're not welcome here!" Then she spit on the ground between the officer's feet and stared him straight in the eye, silently daring him to challenge her.

She was right, the officer admitted to himself. They hadn't presented a warrant and truth be known, they couldn't. The two were on patrol when they received a call to serve the warrant. The officer knew he had no authority to search the premises without presenting a paper warrant and he suspected that Bryant's mother didn't have the authority to allow them access even if she wanted to. It wasn't *her* apartment and she wasn't on the lease.

"Let's go Neil." The cop said.

The officer named Neil nodded and the two left. Mary stood holding her spiteful glare until the squad cars rounded the corner out of sight, then she sighed to herself as she returned to her seat.

A little while later, Lane arrived home. When he entered the apartment complex he spotted the two squad cars but didn't think anything about them. He continued to his apartment, parking in the space marked by his apartment's number. The squad cars, which had been facing the exit to the gated community, each navigated u-turns and fell into pursuit of Lane's truck. By the time the squad cars arrived, Lane had already gotten out of the Chevy and was kneeled in the grass, hugging his sons. The boys, excited to see their father, were climbing on his back and tugging at him to go play with them for awhile.

Lane spotted the two units pulling to a quick stop, one behind his truck to block it in, the other angled in to keep Lane from running in that direction. The cops jumped out of their cruisers immediately pointing their tazers at him.

"Mr. Bryant, we have a warrant for your arrest."

The proclamation shocked Lane, but his shock quickly turned into anger at these *stupid* cops! His sons were crawling all over him *and* he was on his knees.

Lane asked his question with a mixture of amazement and disgust, "What kind of warrant requires you to point those things at my kids!"

Although the tazer was an effective tool for subduing resistant suspects, the voltage that issued from the barbs was enough to kill a child. A wave of nearly uncontrollable rage swept over Lane. At that moment he knew that if he could, he would have wrest the tazers away from those cops, gleefully inserted them into their lower orifices and kept firing until their testicles exploded.

Carol, who stood near Lane's truck, recognized the look on his face and quietly called the children to her and out of any danger from the tazers.

"We have a blue warrant, Mr. Bryant." One of the officers stated flatly.

A blue warrant described a type of warrant issued by the Texas Parole Board in Austin for parolee's who've violated their parole in some way.

"I haven't been off parole for nearly a year! You guys screwed up!" Bryant said incredulously.

"Are you resisting arrest, Mr. Bryant?" came the response.

Bryant looked to his wife and kids taking note of the fear and confusion in their young faces. Carol, nearly in tears, shook her head no.

Bryant slowly raised his hands above his head, "No. No, I'm not resisting. Do your dirt man!"

The officers approached cautiously. "Lie face down on the ground with your hand spread wide." The young officer who'd talked to Lane's mother said in a firm voice.

Lane, still kneeling, obeyed without a word. As soon a he was prone, the officer quickly ran to him, covered by his partner, and landed his knee into Lane's neck holding him down. He quickly hand cuffed Lane then the two pulled him to his feet and escorted him to the patrol car.

Lane was held at Jefferson County Jail in Beaumont, Texas for a week before being extradited to Harris County where he was charged with robbery, a second degree felony.

* * *

Harris County Jail consisted of three buildings of various sizes; the largest of the three could hold as many as seven thousand prisoners at one time. Each of the three buildings were connected to the Harris County courthouse via tunnels which traveled beneath the crowded streets and side walks. There could be any number of prisoners ranging from six hundred to as many as eleven hundred who would be herded to court on any given day. It was a frustrating process for both the prisoners and the guards.

Once the prisoners completed the route to their respective courts, several of them would be packed into hold over rooms which had a metal bench along two walls in an L shape. The opposite wall held a large Plexiglas window sectioned into four stalls by small metal blinds and serviced by a stainless steel table which ran the length of the Plexiglas. The rest of the same wall held two stainless steel toilets and a sink of the same style, separated from the window stalls by a brick wall to prevent the discomfort of the attorneys and other court employees who may otherwise have been forced to witness one of the prisoners in his or her act of excretion.

These rooms were usually packed far beyond the suggested maximum capacity which forced the majority of its unwilling guests to either stand for the five hours they would remain there or sit on the floor at the feet of those who chose to stand.

For six months Lane had sat in this same court holdover, which serviced the courtroom of the Honorable Judge 'Big Time' Bill Rights, several times. His court appointed attorney had thrown every thing he had at Lane to convince him to take a plea bargain for the case against him.

Frustrated, Lane half stood-half stooped at the window because there were no stools to sit on inside the holdover room. Opposite Lane, sitting on a cushioned stool, was Lane's court appointed attorney, a smug look on his face and Lane's folder sitting on the table in front of him.

"Are you fuckin' stupid Martinez? Read my lips. I did *not* rob anybody!" Lane shouted at Martinez who was prepared for the outburst.

He had witnessed several outbursts, from this particular client in the last six months. Lane had been one of Martinez' angrier clients and it seemed that his level of hostility had climbed dramatically in the last few visits, but Martinez recognized that his client's anger had stemmed from fatigue as much as any other reason.

"Well Mr. Bryant, that is very original." Martinez spoke the words with heavy sarcasm. "Why don't you tell me what *really* happened", he continued with an emphasis on the word.

Bryant's expression changed from one of anger and unbridled hatred to one of disgust as he considered the unfolding of events since his arrest in Port Arthur. He had instinctively known at his first meeting with Marcus Martinez that his court appointed attorney wouldn't give him the defense promised to him by law. But then, who could trust the law? Some people felt that the law protected the innocent; others felt that the law only protected the criminals. Lane knew better! The law only protected itself, and any entity that was so self serving could not be trusted. Those who served the law, in Lane's opinion, were nothing more than a type of priest or priestess who sacrificed the innocent on the alter of justice to an evil god. In today's blinded society the ideal of godliness has been distorted; twisted into the 'idol' of selfishness. The truth that these 'priests' and 'priestesses' would tell the people nearly anything they wanted to hear in order to generate votes and campaign 'donations' to protect their careers, is ever hidden by the proclamation of what is righteous and fair to all of Law's subjects.

The rage within Lane's soul began to surface again during his contemplation but he was able to control his expression at this point, showing no emotion at all. Martinez hated this blank expression, it was impossible to read and therefore very difficult to pull the necessary strings within his clients psyche to get his desired response. When faced with this dilemma, Martinez simply waited until Lane spoke. He could do nothing else other than end the meeting, but Martinez wanted this file closed *today*.

In an unnaturally calm, expressionless demeanor Lane spoke, "We've been over this before Martinez. Why are you playing games with me? You've said yourself that this was an easy case to beat! What happened to that?"

"No, Mr. Bryant. I said it *sounded* like an easy case to beat! I hate to admit it, but I was wrong! The assistant D.A. won't come down to a lesser charge. He said that the witness wants you to do some time and he's confident of a win.

"I've warned you about this, Mr. Bryant. It boils down to her word against yours and you being a twice convicted felon I wouldn't advise you to testify.

"Your first conviction of burglary is bad enough, but then you also have the manslaughter offense which proves that you're capable of violence . . ."

Lane cut his attorney off sharply, "That was a long time ago, Martinez! I've served my time and I have a new life now, a good life with a family.

"Besides, I nearly beat that case in trial and the fact that it was dropped to man slaughter testifies to the fact that it was weak. Also, a lot of people on and off the jury felt that what I did was justifiable and . . ."

"And beside the point!" It was Lane's turn to be cut off. "The *conviction* of that trial will be what the jury of *this* trial will ultimately consider, not whether it was justifiable homicide.

"As of now, none of your previous convictions have been mentioned, which makes it a better deal for you. If your indictment had any of the enhancement paragraphs from your priors, you'd be looking at no less than thirty aggravated years; which means you'd serve fifteen calendar years before you could even be considered for parole.

"Understand this, if you take the stand to testify on you own behalf, those priors will definitely come into play. You would have killed yourself. That woman, whether or not she's telling the truth, has never been in jail for *anything*!

"If she takes the stand and starts shedding those tears at the horrific memory of the violation that she endured at *your* hand, and those members of the jury see the tears of this just woman, the law will go right out the window. Emotion will be the deciding factor of this trial and the assistant D.A. will play his violin to the tune of the witness' bleeding heart."

Lane's calm, emotionless expression cracked a little as his inner turmoil raged and rose in its crescendo.

"What about my witness?" Lane asked in short clipped words, betraying his anger. "Doesn't he count for *something*?"

Aside from the hate and frustration at the edges of Lane's voice, Martinez sensed his desperation. Lane would plea bargain and he'd do it *today*.

"How do you think Earnest Moore, a convicted felon and a friend to you, could possible effect your case in a way that would be favorable to you?" Martinez asked with incredulous flare.

Defeated, Lane mumbled more to himself, "I don't know."

Then, in a burst of rage, Lane punched the glass right in front of Martinez, who merely smiled.

Lane growled, "I'm not entirely confident in your representation Martinez. I find it very hard to believe that you've put much effort into my defense or that you've even so much as filed a single motion to help my cause!"

Martinez nodded, "I did indeed file your motions," he lied, "but they were denied."

"On what grounds, Martinez?" Lane yelled through the glass.

Martinez simply shrugged his shoulders, "The judge doesn't need any grounds to deny a motion."

"Man who do you work for?" Lane continued to yell. "First you let them raise my bond an additional thirty grand then you don't even put up a fight to get my fuckin' motions granted and now you want me to give these vultures another fives years of my life! For a fictitious crime, no less!"

Martinez took a long moment to stare hard at his client. This is it, he thought to himself, he's going to sign the plea and accept the offer rather than risk any more time that he might receive at a lost trial. He just needs a little extra push.

Sliding a pen and the plea agreement for five years in the Texas Department of Criminal Justice through a slot at the base of the Plexiglas Martinez spoke to Lane in a saddened tone.

"Sometimes we all have to do things that we don't want to, but we roll with the punches hoping for a better future. If you don't accept the plea, which is entirely your choice, then you could be gone for a much longer time. Then what of your *family*?"

"As I've said before, the prosecuting team believes that a trial could easily be won just on the emotions of the jury alone. When they see that woman start crying, more than likely the law will fly right out the window."

Lane took a moment to go over the plea bargain, the anger of the past six months compiled with the frustration of the injustice he was experiencing and his rage roared within; boiling, rolling and seething just beneath the surface. Violent flashes of murderous visions clicked behind his eyes, dark but enticing promises of vengeance.

There's a point in each person's psyche which should not be exceeded. As Lane felt himself being pushed dangerously close to that explosive point, he could also feel himself being *drawn* to its blissful abyss of indulgence waiting beyond. Lane stood with his eyes closed, trembling. He could barely contain the emotions that engulfed him. His face contorted with rage and hatred as he neared the point of ignition. Voices rose and fell in his ears demanding retribution *now*!

A malevolent voice resounded, cutting through the chaos within. Cold and calculating, it spoke calmly and with great authority, "No need for that here. It serves no purpose now."

Peace. The chaos cut off in an instant as though it had never been. Instantaneously Lane stopped trembling and opened his eyes to glare at Martinez with a steeled hatred that made the attorney's skin prickle. Lane signed the plea bargain and slid it back through the slot to Martinez.

"If one is to uphold the law, Martinez, one must abide by it!" Lane stated in a chilling voice that Martinez had never experienced before.

"What the hell does that mean, Bryant?" Martinez asked, his voice shaking with nervousness.

Lane leaned forward to the glass and with barely a whisper he stated confidently, "I'll get you, you crooked bastards. Every last one of you!"

Chapter Three

AFTER FIVE YEARS in the T.D.C.J. Lane was finally released, having served his entire sentence. He had the opportunity to make parole, but the crimes of his past had not been overlooked by the Texas Board of Pardons and Paroles. In addition, the board felt that Lane had received a lenient sentence, therefore paroled was denied.

Under the new amendment to the parole guidelines in Texas, good time credit and work time credits awarded to offenders of certain crimes could only be applied to parole eligibility and not toward early release, called mandatory supervision. In these cases, an offender either made parole or he served his entire sentence day for day. In the past, if an offender didn't qualify for parole then that offender would be released once his flat time and his good time/work time added together would equal his sentence.

Should an offender violate any of the terms of mandatory supervision then he or she ran the risk of returning to the T.D.C.J. for another term of imprisonment. Most parolees would end up serving time, either on supervision or in prison that dramatically exceeded the original sentence.

DON'T MESS WITH TEXAS!

Lane served his time in what he considered to be slave labor, as he received neither a reduced sentence nor paid wages for worked which he performed *under duress*. A violation of federal slave labor laws.

DON'T MESS WITH TEXAS!

Time! Time that he would not be paid a fair wage for and that can never be replaced. Time Lane used to form his body into a lethal machine which he would need to exact his vengeance on the orchestrators of this injustice.

Patience! Lane had become a master of patience as many prisoners in Texas prisons have. While a lot of the offenders released from the

T.D.C.J. went on sprees of indulgences, Lane kept himself in check when he stepped out of the Walls unit in Huntsville. He held in check the excitement of being free after so long a time. He continually reminded himself that he could never be free until he could retrieve proper retribution for the shit he was forced to endure. The first task at hand would have to be funds, but before he could begin work on that he had to return to his former position as husband and father. The most appealing aspect of his release was the idea of holding his wife and getting to know his boys again.

His return home had been very quiet with the boys, at Carol's insistence, visiting their grandparents.

"I need you for myself, if only for one night." She whispered to Lane.

The couple's reunion had been astronomical, at least for Lane, for the two expressed five years of pent up sexual desires in the long awaited and greatly anticipated rejoining. Lane's faithful wife had remained chaste and true to their marriage and Lane admired her for that. Secretly he wondered if he could have remained as faithful as her had she been in prison. During the first encounter, Carol had shown her dramatic prowess, unleashing her desires with the passion of a goddess.

Soft, uncertain caresses, such as displayed by nervous teenagers had been the initial foreplay. But that had quickly given way to the animalistic acts portrayed in some of the newer, more offensive pornography films of this generation. Even after Lane had been spent Carol continued on and wanting to please his deserving mate, Lane denied his own fatigue and pushed himself forward. Insatiable for what seemed to Lane to be an eternity, Carol demanded that she be taken in ways far beyond the dreams that Lane had indulged himself with during their separation. Draining the last drop of Lane's lust and finally satisfying her own, Carol fell limp onto her lover's chest with the groan of an explosive orgasm that left her legs shaking. Peacefully and quietly, the two slept in one another's arms content and very much in love.

The boys arrived home the following day and it was a happy reunion. The family spent the afternoon at the park playing touch football and that evening they all went out for a nice family dinner. With all the excitement and all the love he felt that day, Lane had nearly reconsidered all that he spent the last few years planning for.

Nearly!

* * *

During the next several months, Lane implemented the idea that would finance his war. Using the internet, Lane was able to acquire several identities from which he stole several thousands of dollars each. He kept using different people's resources to add to his arsenal of cash which he kept in different safe deposit boxes in many locations throughout Port Arthur, Beaumont and even Houston. Lane even went so far as to keep a duffle bag full of fifties and hundreds in a locker at the Greyhound bus station near downtown Houston. He built his balance up to almost one hundred-fifty thousand dollars, using other's money. Soon he was making Texas state driver's license with pictures of himself in various disguises, using a digital camera and some materials that were rather difficult to obtain.

One evening after his family went to bed he was working on the I.D.s at his computer when Carol entered the living room.

"Whatcha doing, baby?" She asked, drawing out the words in an innocent and sweet voice that immediately sent Lane into thoughts of erotica.

"Oh, nothin' really. I was playing a couple of games of chess online, but I was just about to come to bed." Lane replied, a wry grin spread across his face.

Carol crossed the room, wearing a slightly see-through white nightgown that hung just below her thong panties. Her hard nipples were very visible through the thin fabric. She sat in Lane's lap, wiggling her bottom enticingly against her 'toy' tucked away in her husband's pants, commanding its attention and Lane didn't disappoint. She smiled devilishly when she felt his erection through his jeans. Snaking her arms around his neck, she continued to wiggle her bottom slowly in his lap.

Butterflies instantly invaded Lane's stomach, making him tremble and forcing a lump to get lodged in his throat. He was amazed at how this beautiful woman he knew so well . . . so intimately, could still have this kind of effect on him. He was giddy. Whatever the spell this sexy lady had over him, Lane liked it and once again he found himself reconsidering the course that he set before him.

"Why don't you come to bed with me?" Carol asked with her most seductive voice.

She spoke with her lips against Lane's neck, just below his ear, brushing lightly on his skin. Lane managed a nod and a barely audible "Ok." escaped his lips, as he allowed his wife to lead him to bed.

* * *

Lane had spent many, many nights since his plea bargain trying to decide who would be the first. One name kept coming to him again and again, and one question above all stood out. He had to know why Vikki Roberts would do what she did to him. *WHY!*

Questioning her, or any of the people which he had mentally listed to face his wrath, would be very risky. It meant that he would have to reveal himself; but isn't that what he wanted? It was a question Lane asked himself many times. Of course he wanted his victims to know who he was and why he was doing the things he was doing.

That line of thinking usually brought about another question; could he call these people victims? Of course, today's society would label them as such but then today's society was blinded to the crimes that these people committed. No. Lane would no longer call these people victims. From this day forward they would be referred to as offenders, the same as Lane was referred to for the five years that they had him locked up.

Through his investigations on the web, Lane had gained home and work addresses of all the offenders home and work addresses as well as their vehicle descriptions and their license plate numbers. He saved the info to a flash drive that was well hidden in his truck, in case he needed it for future reference.

Lane had lied to Carol about a job he had landed to cover for the time spent gathering the funds needed to track and confront the offenders. The job was insurance estimates on residential roofs. It required him to travel a bit and it paid cash per job. He hated lying to Carol but he needed a cover for his frequent nights away and the extra cash he brought home from his thefts helped that cover go over easily.

* * *

The January nearly one full year after Lane's release found him sitting in a camaro outside a small restaurant whose sign boasted the best steak fajitas in south Houston. The camaro was bought used and registered under the name 'Dirk Diggler'. This was a little humor on Lane's part. Dirk Diggler was the stage name for a porn star in the movie 'Boogie Nights'. When Lane made this fake I.D. he thought to himself, 'someone is definitely gonna get fucked!'

Lane fitted suppressors onto the barrels onto the two nine millimeter pistols purchased earlier that day and placed them into their adapted holsters which he wore on each hip. He slid into a dark jacket bearing a cable TV logo and placed a matching cap low over his brow. He stood outside the camaro checking his appearance in the reflection of the door's window, making sure that the jacket he wore hid the extended barrels of the suppressed pistols.

Satisfied, he weaved several eighteen inch long zip cords through his belt loops. Grabbing the clipboard he brought to complete his disguise he headed down the street to the side of the restaurant. Lane walked in a round about route through the neighborhood, monitoring the houses he passed as he made his way to Vikki Roberts' home. Most people were indoors on the cold January evening so Lane was confident that no one would take any notice of him. Arriving at Roberts' home he approached the front door while unbuttoning his jacket and releasing the holster clasps, making his weapons accessible. With a gloved hand he pressed the doorbell and pretended to look over some paperwork on his clipboard. Lane heard the locks disengage and as soon as the door began to swing inward, he kicked hard at the space just below the doorknob forcing it open with enough power to jerk the security chain from the door jam and splinter the wood. The woman who answered the door was knocked to the floor. Lane moved fast in the foyer and, shutting the door behind, placed a solid kick to her chin.

In one fluid motion he withdrew one of the suppressed nine mm. pistols in his right hand and engaged the door's deadbolt with his left. He grabbed the woman by her hair, recognizing her as Vikki Roberts.

Lifting her head off the floor Lane growled, "Who else is here bitch?" his eyes focused on the room beyond the foyer.

No answer came. Infuriated, Lane smashed the butt of his pistol into Roberts' forehead knocking her unconscious then he moved boldly deeper into the house. Lane caught a glint of reflected light heading toward his head. Had the heavy metallic bat been aimed at his mid section, Lane might not have been able to move out of its way in time. However, the club swung high enough for Lane to easily duck under its deadly arch, losing no ground or momentum in his progression.

Slightly altering his direction, Lane stepped into the threat and, grabbing the man at the back of his head, drove a vicious head-butt across the bridge of his attacker's nose. He repeated the head-butt just for good measure then quickly followed the double strike by stomping with all of his might and weight onto the inside of the man's left knee, breaking it with an audible '*pop*'. With that threat incapacitated Lane pulled his second pistol and continued with his inspection.

Deeper into the family room a dining room branched off to the left and beyond that, a kitchen. On the far side of the kitchen stood an older woman, phone in one hand, frozen with fear and staring wide-eyed at Lane.

"I can put a bullet in your right eye from here so quietly that you wouldn't even hear it." Lane calmly stated then fired a round into the wall, inches from the woman's head.

The woman didn't flinch until she heard the impact at the wall next to her, then she jerked so hard that her head knocked the wall behind her and she dropped the phone with a yelp.

"Hang up that damn phone!" Lane demanded.

The woman just stood in place, crying. "I said *now!*" Lane yelled, causing the woman to flinch violently.

She did as she was told, crying uncontrollably.

"Shut the fuck up! You're not dead yet." Lane said his voice full of venom.

Keeping the pistol in his right hand aimed at the woman, Lane took one step backward into the family room, pointing the pistol in his left hand at the man who had the bat. He was crawling toward the door where Vikki Roberts lay unconscious. Lane fired once into the man's elbow, destroying it and sending him flat on his face. The man began cursing and growling threats through clenched teeth.

"Shut up, punk!" Lane told the man, "That was my left hand; I was aiming for your heart. You're lucky to be breathing!"

To the woman Lane demanded, "Is anybody else here?"

The woman shook her head, streams of tears running down her cheeks.

"Good!" he continued, "Get over here and bring three of those chairs with you."

The woman at first didn't respond, so Lane fired another round into the same wall near her head. Again she jerked violently but then did as Lane had instructed. She brought the chairs to him then helped the man who'd been shot into one and secured him with the zip cords. Holstering one of his weapons, Lane secured the older woman to a chair then Vikki Roberts as well.

Lane made a quick inspection through the rest of the house and connecting garage, bringing back with him a two gallon fuel can full of gas. Tired of the trio's questions, Lane took some dish towels from the kitchen using them to gag the man and older woman. Retrieving a fourth chair from the dining room, Lane sat in front of Vikki Roberts glaring at her but not speaking. Finally recognition flashed in Roberts' eyes.

"So you do remember me?" Lane asked.

A simple nod was all the answer Roberts would give.

"Well, it's good that you know. In fact, that's the main point of all this." Lane waved his hand toward the other two captives.

Without warning, or any indication that he'd do so, Lane grabbed a handful of Roberts' hair and violently jerked her head back so that her neck popped into a painful angle and her face shown upward.

Lane put his lips next to her ear and quietly whispered, "Its judgment day bitch!"

Roberts' eyes filled with tears knowing that there'd be no one to save her. Again, without warning, Lane twisted her neck to near breaking. The sudden shift in pressure caused a pain filled yelp to escape her lips.

"Who the hell is that?" Lane demanded to know, pointing at the bound man.

"He's my . . . my brother." Roberts gasped and stuttered.

Once more Lane jerked her head back then released her and took his seat in front of her.

"Five fuckin' years! In that time the only question that I could think to ask is, *why?*"

Confused, Roberts simply stared at Lane. Her silence lasted a moment longer than Lane could tolerate. Exploding forward he drove a mighty fist into Roberts' mouth, snapping her head back.

"*WHY!* Goddamn you!" he demanded.

Nearly unconscious from the blow, Roberts just let her head droop forward. Blood flowed freely onto her lap and, after a time, she spit out a couple of broken teeth.

Eventually her head cleared and she began to whimper as she spoke, "He made me say all those things. He said my statement had to guarantee a conviction. He practically wrote the statement *himself* then forced me to sign it."

"Who's *he?*" Lane demanded to know.

"Detective Osbourne." was the whimpered reply.

Lane knew the name. Osbourne came to visit him with Detective Von Eric before his court date, trying to elicit some form of confession from him. Lane agreed to meet with the two detectives hoping that he could convince them that there had been a mistake. Of course Lane had no such luck. He realized the futility of it all when he spotted a recorder hidden under a couple of files during the visit.

"Are you recording this meeting?" Lane asked infuriated.

Knowing that fact could no longer be hidden, Osbourne answered with a simple, "Yes."

"You're supposed to inform me if you're gonna do that!" Lane said furiously.

"No. We don't have to inform *you* of *anything*."

"This interview is over." Lane said. "You can talk to my lawyer if you have any more questions."

"Oh, we already have Mr. Bryant." Osbourne said with a smirk. "And we will again."

That last statement stuck with Lane for years. Often he'd wondered exactly what the detective meant by that last statement. Lane now remembered Von Eric's demeanor during that interview. The junior detective never said a word; he simply stood behind his partner with an unpleasant frown on his face. Lane could see Von Eric's expression clearly in his mind's eye.

In a softer tone than before, Lane asked, "What about Von Eric?"

Barely able to shake her drooping hair, Roberts said, "He didn't say much, other than hello and goodbye. He just sat on the edge of the table while I gave my statement and stared at me and Detective Osbourne."

"That's it? Nothin' else?" Lane prodded once more.

Roberts lifted her head to face Lane. A look of remembrance slowly crept across her face, as though she had just remembered something of vital importance.

"He warned about filing a false report."

"But you did it anyway!" Lane spat, anger filling his voice again.

The flow of blood from Roberts' lips slowed to a near stop, but that only seemed to increase the throbbing pain.

"Osbourne told you to lie and you did! Why?" Lane demanded to know the truth.

Not giving Roberts the chance to answer, he continued on, "How could he even know about me without you telling him in the first place!" it was more a statement than a question.

Lane knew Roberts was hiding something. In an instant, he jumped to his feet and slapped Roberts hard across her cheek. Lane had her by the throat before the flash of white light receded from her vision, squeezing her esophagus between his fingers and thumb.

Lane's voice filled with rage. "I asked you a question you lying fuck!" he growled, applying pressure to Roberts' throat. "You better give me a straight answer or I'll kill your whole fuckin' family! In fact . . ."

Instead of finishing the sentence he released his captive's throat, who immediately began gasping for air. He stormed toward the man across the room, withdrawing one of the suppressed weapons as he went. Without a pause Lane leveled the weapon at a point right between the man's wide eyes.

"Tell your brother bye!" Lane spat then squeezed the trigger.

The impact of the bullet caused the man's head to snap back with such force that the front legs of the chair he was bound to lifted off the floor. His ruined head rocked forward again but the chair continued its tilt back. Time seemed to slow as the chair teetered on its hind legs before crashing backward. The impact to the hard wood floor sent whatever matter was left in the cadaver's head splattering in all directions. Time returned to its normal continuance as the red spray of blood and brains, sent airborne by the bullet, began to settle.

Full of vehemence Lane returned to Roberts, grabbing her hair and again jerking her head back forcefully. He placed the hot metal of the gun's barrel against the tender skin of her exposed throat, searing it. A slight odor of burnt flesh reached Lane's nose, feeding his bloodlust.

"I've got seven more rounds in this gun, you lying cunt, where you want 'em!" Lane growled with such rage that spittle flew into Roberts' battered and bloodied face.

"One hundred and twenty thousand." Roberts cried uncontrollably, on the verge of hysteria.

"What?!" Lane was caught off guard.

He hadn't expected Roberts to say anything. Especially anything that had to do with paying him not to kill her. The insult fueled his rage and he struck her again, this time with the back of his gloved hand.

"I don't need your money, bitch!" then he struck her again.

"No! Please!" Roberts cried, tears freely flowing down her bruised cheeks. "That was the payoff. One hundred and twenty thousand dollars."

Lane was shocked out of his raged filled episode. "What're you talking about? Why would anyone pay you to send *me* to prison?"

The confusion Lane was feeling calmed him a little.

"No one *paid* me, we collected insurance on some valuables you were blamed for stealing. Then we collected some more from an organization Detective Osbourne introduced me to." Roberts whimpered through her sobs.

Lane returned to his seat and watched her cry for awhile. After her fit subsided Lane continued his questioning. This time his tone was casual.

"So you used me to collect insurance money. Where is it then?"

Roberts sniffed her leaking nose as she spoke. "Osbourne has it. Or *had* it. I don't know . . . He took it from me! He *made* me do it, don't you see? I had no choice!"

Lane shook his head solemnly. "I could have taught you to make hundreds of thousands of dollars through the internet, if you were just looking for a scam. But instead you felt that you had to send me to prison.

"There's no way for you to repay me for that lost time, Vikki. The way I see it is you, Osbourne and everyone else involved in sending me away, owe me. How can you possible pay me back for the time I've lost? Time that *you've* stolen from me."

Roberts shook her head pleadingly. "Please. I *had* to! He *made* me!"

"Shhh!" Lane made the noise quietly. "You can't give back what you've helped to take, so I'll have to be a little creative with *your* sentencing."

Lane paused for a moment in a mock pose of contemplation. Looking over his shoulder at the dead man on the floor Lane said in a low voice, "I could say that he has paid for your part in all this, but that really wouldn't be very just, would it. After all nobody took *my* place when I was sentenced to prison."

Roberts began to cry again when Lane turned to face her.

"Unfortunately for you, Vikki, I am not a very creative person. I can't think of anyway that you might make amends, so . . ."

Slowly Lane raised the pistol, aiming it at Roberts' chest.

Shaking her head frantically, Roberts started to beg, "No . . . Please . . ." but she was cut off by three nine mm. rounds fired into her chest.

Lane took a short moment to watch her die then approached his last captive. The older woman remained wide-eyed and unmoving.

In a sympathetic voice, Lane explained "I really do apologize. I don't know who you are or if you had any part in this mess, but either way you've gotta go."

Lane raised his weapon to the woman's face but she remained completely still. Her wide-eyed face was frozen in shock. She didn't squirm, whine or blink, and for the first time Lane noticed the emptiness in her eyes. He poked the end of the suppressor into one of them but got no response. The woman was dead.

"Incredible!" Lane mumbled to himself.

Instead of trying to remove any evidence that could be tied to him, Lane doused the bodies with the gas from the garage. He turned his jacket inside out, stuffed his cap into a pocket and tied a bandana around his head. He lit the gas and left the house through the back and into the ally, returning to Mr. Diggler's camaro. Hurrying away from the area and circling downtown Houston on I 610 loop he stopped only once, atop the bridge that crossed the Intercoastal Canal near the Port of Houston. Lane put the jacket, cap, bandana, weapons and holsters into a light vinyl nap sac, discarding the items over the side of the bridge into the canal far below.

Once in Beaumont, Lane sank the camaro to the bottom of a very large private pond, retrieved his truck and was home just after midnight.

* * *

"Hello?" Von Eric mumbled from his sleep.

"Rise and shine Enis." Came an insistent voice through the phone's speaker. "We've got a triple whammy on the south side. It's ugly too, so you may want to skip breakfast. You need to get here pretty quick anyway, before the clean up boys trample the place."

Von Eric cracked his eyelids to peer at the soft glow of the digital clock placed on his bedside table. Two thirteen am.

"Damn." The junior detective croaked miserably.

Rolling onto his side, Von Eric fumbled for the pen and notepad that he kept next to the clock.

"Ok norm, give me the address." He said, using the illumination of the clock to see. He paused for a moment then sighed. "Alright, I'll be there ASAP." Ending the call with a groan he forced himself out of bed.

It took Von Eric forty minutes to arrive to the scene. Standing in what was left of a once cozy family room he listened to senior Detective Norman Fitzgerald highlight the facts. Fitzgerald stood nearly six inches shorter than his younger partner. His crinkled dress shirt was adorned with a fresh coffee stain. He had long since removed his tie and his salt and peppered hair was a mess from him constantly running his fingers through it.

Reading from his notepad Fitzgerald ran through the information with mechanical indifference. "Of the three bodies only one was male. And one of the two females seemed to have been left to die in the fire."

Fitzgerald pointed to the corpse with the large hole in its head. "That's the male. Looks like he took a hollow-point slug at close range.

"This one here," Fitzgerald pointed to the remains of Vikki Roberts. "She seems to be the intended target."

Von Eric cut in, "Not a robbery then." it was more a statement than a question.

Shaking his head Fitzgerald continued, "Hell no! At least *I'd* say it wasn't a robbery. Look at that victim's chest."

Von Eric squatted near the body as Fitzgerald pointed to the wounds.

"Three rounds Enis, center mass." After a short pause Fitzgerald continued, "Execution style."

Von Eric stood and, looking at his partner, he said "So give me your take Norm."

"Well, that's just it; an execution. For some reason, somebody wanted this one dead. That one," Fitzgerald indicated the male corpse "was probably killed to make a point. If so, then I'd have to conclude that the target was interrogated before she was killed."

"What about that victim?" Von Eric nodded, indicating the other female.

"To be honest, I don't have a clue. There's no bullet wounds, it doesn't make any sense to me. All I can figure is she was left to die in the fire."

Von Eric asked "Is it possible that a professional hit man would leave behind a potential witness with even the smallest possibility to survive the fire and then identify him?"

Detective Fitzgerald was already shaking his head. "I never said it was a *professional* anything Enis. No professional would light a fire *after* he killed his mark. Maybe he would use a fire to kill the target, you know, to make it look like an accident. A fire started in this fashion would just create a beacon. It would draw our attention, that's not how a professional would handle it."

"Ok, Norm." Von Eric said with a yawn. "Do we have any names yet?"

Again the senior detective shook his head. "No names on the victims yet but the house belongs to Emilio Roberts, deceased. He was survived by a wife, Kaitlyn, and two children, Vincent and Victoria."

"Vikki Roberts?" Von Eric asked incredulously.

Fitzgerald eyed his partner. "You know her?"

Nodding slowly, Von Eric answered honestly. "I helped to handle a robbery complaint that she filed sometime back. A very nervous type she was."

"Well," Fitzgerald said solemnly, "If she's here, she ain't nervous anymore."

Von Eric stood in silence for a long moment. Then after seeming to come to a decision he looked to his partner.

"Norm, I'd like to go with the bodies and speak to the coroner."

"Sure Enis, something on your mind?"

Shaking his head, Von Eric replied, "If it turns out that one of the victims *is* Vikki Roberts, then I'll be coming to work late tomorrow."

Curiosity perked Fitzgerald to attention. "Really?" He asked unhappily.

Quickly Von Eric assured him, "It has no bearing on this case, Norm. I'm just showing a professional courtesy that's all."

* * *

At seven am that same morning Von Eric pounded on a decorative oak door. There had been no answer so far but he heard some soft mumblings and cursings from within the brick walls. Raising his fist to pound on the door again Von Eric heard the lock disengage. The door opened to reveal a haggard looking Osbourne with messed hair and stubbled beard.

"Don't tell me you've stopped by to wish me luck with my ensuing battle." Osbourne's tone was drenched in sarcasm.

"I wouldn't want to do that Dave. After all you make your own luck, isn't that right."

"Well if this is going to take awhile, you might as well come in, even though you're not welcome. I'm not going to stand out here in the cold to listen to some shit I probably wouldn't care less about. Just don't get too comfortable, Enis, I may throw you out faster than you might be thinking."

Osbourne talked over his shoulder as he receded back into his expensively decorated and immaculately clean abode. Most people might wonder how a detective in Houston could fill a home with furnishings such as these, or even have a home of this eloquence, but Von Eric knew that the former detective's *unofficial* activities had provided him with these luxuries. He knew but even after eighteen months of investigating Osbourne, he could prove none of the illegal activities. Furthermore, Osbourne's extra income could all be accounted for by various real estate investments.

Von Eric knew it was all bullshit, but proving it had itself proven to be a most difficult task. He had finally given up the investigation when his sister had a horrific car wreck with her two small children in the car with her. Later a message showed up in his email that there are no such things as accidents.

Von Eric followed Osbourne to the kitchen near the rear of the house. Osbourne went straight to fixing himself a glass of Hennessy.

"I'd offer you something to drink Enis," he stated flatly as he turned to face Von Eric, "but I hate your guts!" he finished by raising the glass to his lips.

The feeling is mutual Von Eric thought to himself, but withheld the spiteful remark. Instead he focused on his reason for coming in the first place.

"We found three bodies in a burned down house early this morning Dave on the south side."

I'm not a detective any more Enis, haven't you heard?" Osbourne said, slamming his glass to the counter and pouring another three finger drink. "If I was, homicide is not my department." He finished, staring hard at his former partner.

"Precisely why I transferred there." The words leaped out before Von Eric could catch them.

Osbourne raised his glass in toast, "Here's to small favors then." He drained the glass, again slamming it down to the counter.

After a long silence Osbourne finally said, "Surely there's more to your visit than that Enis."

Nodding Von Eric said, "We think one of the deceased was targeted in an execution. She was shot three times in her chest before she was burned in an arson."

Osbourne placed his right hand on the counter near his empty glass, rested the thumb of his right hand against his temple with his fingers on the other and lightly massaged his forehead.

With his eyes closed, Osbourne asked, "Enis, why should I give a damn?"

"We think the target is Vikki Roberts. Remember her Dave? You helped her with that trumped up affidavit on the last case we worked together. I checked this morning; Bryant has been released for almost a year now, after serving his entire sentence."

Osbourne gaped at Von Eric during the whole revelation. When he finished Osbourne rolled his eyes, dramatically motioning with his hands.

"*SO*! I'm supposed to care about any of this shit? Let me bring you up to date, Detective Von Eric. I'm dying from cancer. It's likely I'll be dead before it's discovered who *did* kill Ms. Roberts. It's the reason I took an early retirement, so I can die in peace, without those headaches that come with the job. Now that's all the patience I have for you cop, get out!"

Von Eric nodded and turned to leave.

At the front door he looked back to Osbourne, "If Bryant did kill Roberts, he may be seeking vengeance. If that's the case then you're the one responsible for getting her killed."

Von Eric opened the door and left not bothering to shut it behind himself. Osbourne strode purposefully through the open door onto the porch.

"I didn't make that woman file a complaint, Enis." He shouted down to Von Eric.

Von Eric stopped and without turning to face toward his former partner, said "No, you didn't. You just made her lie about what actually happened."

And with that, Von Eric got into his car and drove back to the station, thinking the whole way about how healthy Osbourne appeared to be for someone dying of cancer.

* * *

Back at the station Von Eric discovered that his partner was out pumping the Roberts' neighbors for information to help in the case. At his computer Von Eric familiarized himself with Bryant again. He noted an old cell phone number belonging to Carol Bryant and wondered if the couple's marriage had survived his trip to prison. Von Eric dialed the number and was surprised to discover that it wasn't disconnected.

He was even more surprised when an attractive voice answered, "This is Carol."

"Mrs. Bryant?" Von Eric managed.

"Yes. Who's calling?"

"This is detective . . ." the line went dead. Confused, Von Eric redialed the number.

"Hello?" Carol asked in a frustrated tone.

"Mrs. Bry . . ."

"Look detective," Carol interrupted rudely, "I don't know why you're calling my cell phone and unless it's some kind of emergency involving my family I've got nothing to say to you. Is there an emergency involving my family, detective?"

"No ma'am. I . . ." again he was cut short.

"It's been my experience, detective, that anytime an officer of the law just wants to talk, what that officer is really trying to do is find an excuse to arrest the innocent. But I'd be more than happy to tell you to 'go to hell' to your face just as soon as you can deliver a warrant to me for my inspection. Good day detective." Then the line went dead again.

Von Eric just stared blankly at the hand set he'd been trying to talk into. He was at a loss and for the first time thought he may have just been paranoid about Roberts' death.

* * *

Lane jogged to the corner store, purchased a Houston Chronicle then sprinted back to his apartment, as he did every morning at home. After his morning jog and workout Lane took a shower then cooked breakfast for his family, who'd be awake soon. As he ate he read about the death of the Roberts family. He relaxed some when he read that there were no suspects, he assumed that he'd be at the top of the list.

"Good morning, baby." Carol scooted into the small dining room where Lane sat reading the paper.

Leaning down to kiss him she asked, "Anything good in the paper today?"

"Just the same old negativity." Lane smiled, "What'd you expect from Houston?"

"Then why do read it?" Carol asked as she went into the kitchen to get herself a cup of coffee.

"I don't know. Just curious I guess. I keep expecting some type of catastrophe to hit there, maybe a comet will wipe out that god forsaken place. Besides, it gives me a reason to run every morning."

Lane looked over to his wife and thought to himself how naturally beautiful she was. Right there, at that moment she was more beautiful than any model that'd spent a small fortune on nips and tucks or lifts and implants.

Folding the paper closed and rising from his chair Lane asked, "Can you get the boys up and goin' this morning? I want to do a little surfin' on the net before the day starts."

"Sure baby." Carol answered, lifting her face to return Lane's kiss.

While his family ate the breakfast he'd prepared and got ready for the day ahead, Lane reviewed the archives of Houston's local news stations. One title in particular caught his attention, 'Decorated Officer Detective Dave Osbourne Retires'.

Lane stared at the article for a long moment before mumbling to himself, "What're you planning Osbourne?"

Lane clicked the video icon next to the title so he could view the coverage. The story went on about the former detective's distinguished career and his outstanding arrest/conviction record, but never gave any indication why the detective had decided to take an early retirement. Lane logged on to the website for the Houston Chronicle and began reviewing issues as far back as twenty four months before discovering that former detective Dave Osbourne was inflicted with cancer.

Osbourne was quoted saying, "The treatment for this disease is physically too much to allow me to continue in this line of work effectively. Therefore, regretfully, I must take retirement early. However, I have full confidence in the capabilities and competence of the men and women of the Houston Police Department. Houston is in good hands."

Lane reread the statement several times. "Oh no you don't Osbourne." Lane mumbled to himself. "Cop or no cop, you've been found guilty and have been sentenced to death . . . and I shall come quickly."

Chapter Four

THAT AFTERNOON LANE drove to Beaumont, a small city bordering the outskirts of Port Arthur. Just a fraction of the size of Houston, Beaumont was still a very busy, very crowded area for its size. Lane withdrew several thousand in cash from one of his many safe deposit boxes. The next day he would be leaving for 'work' so he wanted to take the family out for a night on the town. He picked the boys up from school and helped with their homework, then took them shopping for new clothes.

He did keep a close eye on his spending, not wanting to alarm his wife or raise any suspicion about the money's source. All four men, young and old, waited at Lane's truck outside the building where Carol worked. Each of the four wore fresh hair cuts; new suits with colorful ties and held roses matching their ties, Carol's favorite.

"Look at you guys." She exclaimed, "You all look like such gentlemen!"

Carol received the flowers from her boys, kissing them each in turn. Her eyes were gleaming when she stood in front of Lane.

"Is all this for me?" she asked, wrapping her husband in a long embrace, kissing him passionately.

"Mmm . . ." was all Lane could manage for a moment. Then he quietly whispered, "I hope you're not too tired to allow these three fine boys and myself to escort you to dinner."

"Who could deny such a request from gentlemen as handsome as you four?" Carol stated with dramatic flare.

After dinner Carol's weariness was apparent and the youngest of the boys had fallen asleep in the truck. Instead of ruining the night by pushing his family to spend more time out in the lights of the small city, Lane opted for a couple of movie rentals instead; Carol having stated that she'd rather relax at home with a good movie . . . and a foot massage. Of course Lane wouldn't deny her something so simple, she deserved as much . . . and more.

It was bad enough that Lane had to deceive her about what he'd been doing at 'work', and he felt more than a little guilty about the deceit. He tried to make up for it by showering her with extra attention which she soaked up greedily, never suspecting that her husband was anything more or less than he claimed to be. Lane longed for the day when his business would be finished but he couldn't let the matter go unchecked. He couldn't force himself to let go the people who unjustly sent him away. His demon would never allow it.

The following morning as Lane prepared to return to Houston, he considered his course and his remaining victims. There's that word again, Lane thought to himself. He didn't understand why he kept referring to them as his victims, *he* was *their* victim! *He* was the one who was robbed! They were no longer victims, Lane reminded himself again. They've been charged and condemned but their sentence holds no prison or cells . . . or future. Their cells will be coffins . . . their prison, hell!

During his drive to Houston, Lane's thought dwelt on how to best deal with the terminally ill former detective. Lane figured that Osbourne's pension wouldn't pay in full because of his early retirement and if he had any insurance, the premium probably skyrocketed if it didn't drop him altogether. Also, Lane figured, the detective was losing a fight with a very painful disease. And finally, the detective has children.

Of all the various avenues from which death could befall Osbourne, one rang out above them all . . . Suicide.

* * *

Former Detective Dave Osbourne sat patiently on the examination table at the cancer clinic where it was believed the he had been receiving treatment for cancer. Osbourne hadn't given much thought to Von Eric's unannounced and unwelcome visit in the previous week. However, he did consider the possibilities that could arise if Bryant was indeed seeking some sort of revenge. If Osbourne was lucky, and he usually was, Bryant would end up helping him more than hurting him.

Osbourne's contemplation was interrupted when the door of the examination room swung inward, a doctor follow it.

"Morning Mr. Osbourne." the doctor said cheerily, perching himself on the edge of a swivel top stool and opening the file in his hand.

"Cut the shit Zeppelin!" Osbourne said. "Did you take care of your business?"

"Did you bring my cash, Dave?" Zeppelin shot back.

Osbourne reached into the inner breast pocket of his sports coat, withdrawing an envelope of large bills and tossed it to the waiting doctor. Dr. Zeppelin stood about five and a half feet tall with a round, full gut and slouched shoulders. His head full of wild hair and his thick mustache was mostly grey with a little of some darker color, giving him an appearance similar to Albert Einstein.

Dr. Zeppelin thumbed the bills. "That's very good Dave. *Very* good! Yes, you're all set to meet your maker and nobody'll be the wiser. The coroner is expecting you when ever you get ready, there's only one thing we haven't discussed yet."

Osbourne had been caught off guard but recovered quickly. As he stared at the old doctor and could only imagine that their deal had just taken a turn for the worst.

"What could that be?" Osbourne asked innocently, suspecting the answer.

"Well, we've got your death taken care of and for another seventy five thousand a year, you get to stay dead. I call it my retirement fund but I guess you could call it blackmail."

Osbourne suspected as much. Showing his best smile, Osbourne stood. "Is this a deal that you put together yourself or are there others expecting payment as well?"

"No. no, just me. Everyone else is quite content with the money they've been given, which is better for the both of us don't you think?" Dr. Zeppelin finished with a smug look on his face, watching Osbourne walk toward the door.

Osbourne turned to face the sitting M.D., a wicked grin spread across his features replacing the smile he wore only seconds earlier.

"Fair enough doc. I'll give you what you deserve."

Just as Zeppelin allowed his smile to show, Osbourne crossed the short distance from the door so fast that the doctor couldn't even get to his feet. Osbourne's shoe crunched into Zeppelin's face, flattening the doctor's nose and breaking his outdated black plastic framed glasses. Zeppelin fell backward, splitting his head on the hard tiled floor. A broken piece of his plastic glasses stabbed into his right eye. Trying to pull the object out of his eye only caused the whole organ to pop out of its socket but before he could scream in horror, Osbourne was on the attack.

Stomping with all his power Osbourne pounded the downed man repeatedly until he heard the 'pop' of the doctor's breaking neck. Osbourne grabbed the fifty thousand dollars, hid the body in the space behind a solid examination table, cleaned the room and stuffed his file under his shirt then left the clinic in the calm and saddened demeanor of a cancer victim.

* * *

Lane waited patiently for the former detective to approach his sedan parked in the large lot outside the cancer clinic. Lane had arrived at Osbourne's home to see him exiting his house. Pulling into the driveway of a nearby property Lane watched the man leave followed him from a safe distance. Osbourne led him to Houston's medical district on the south west side of downtown. Lane was unsure how he could *force* the former detective to swallow the poison. Acquiring the poison that morning was more trouble than Lane cared to bother with. His contact wasn't too happy either when he learned that Lane only wanted as small a purchase as this one, but the extra two thousand Lane offered helped to smooth things over.

While Lane watched the parking lot outside the clinic he thought maybe he'd just have to put two rounds into Osbourne's head and be done with him. But that might inadvertently bring an investigation to his doorsteps, should the connection between Osbourne and Roberts ever be uncovered. The sight of Osbourne's exit from the medical building brought Lane out of his contemplation. He stood next to a large pickup truck, shielding himself from the security cameras, and watched Osbourne through the vehicle's tinted windows. Once the former detective passed Lane's position, he filed in a few parking spaces behind. Lane took his time in the pursuit allowing Osbourne to retrieve his keys and use the remote to unlock the doors.

"Don't move detective, and if that car alarm goes off I'll kill you where you stand. Then I'll kill your kids, your two daughters, just for the headache you've given me!" Lane whispered just loud enough for Osbourne to hear from the short distance.

"Bryant?" Osbourne asked flatly.

Lane was shocked at hearing his own name. Could he have already been discovered, he wondered to himself, but how so fast.

Osbourne took the silence as an affirmation to his half question. "What do you want Mr. Bryant?" he went on to inquire.

Lane's panic mounted, they already suspected him, before he even really begun. The panic triggered a multitude of thoughts ringing audibly in his ears, causing his confusion to intensify dramatically. Lane took a step back, rocked by his inner turmoil. Osbourne slowly turned to face his aggressor only to be met with a powerful kick to his groin, doubling him over. Lane hadn't even realized he moved until the detective had fallen to the concrete. Now totally aware of his actions but unable to control them, Lane 'watched' himself search Osbourne for any weapons.

Satisfied the downed man was weaponless; Lane listened as a calm voice, uncharacteristic of his raging panic, spoke to the downed man. "I want you to get into the car a drive detective!" Lane opened both driver's side doors. "Get up you piece of trash. Get in the fuckin' car!" Lane heard himself growl.

Osbourne picked himself up and slid into the driver's seat, Lane sat in the seat directly behind him.

"I have a gun pointed at you at all times, any shit out of you and I kill you, then I kill your kids!" Lane bluffed.

Lane would never hurt any child, but Osbourne had no idea what he was capable of and therefore followed Lane's instructions carefully. The former detective was panicked himself, everything was in place for him to fake his own death but it might all be for nothing if he couldn't find his way out of this situation.

He wasn't very optimistic about his possibilities. "Well, you've got me Mr. Bryant. Now what?"

"Get out of here and get on 610. How much gas do you have?"

"Three quarters."

"Good." Lane replied. "That'll give us some time to talk."

Lane directed his captive through his chosen route to interstate highway 610. Although 610 is considered an interstate highway it never left the state. In fact it never left Houston; it just made one big loop around downtown. Lane had chosen this highway to give him time to think. Osbourne knew who he was immediately, had expected him even. Lane's options had been dramatically reduced and he started to think to himself that he was all but convicted.

"Are you goin' to tell me what this is all about, Mr. Bryant?" Osbourne asked, drawing Lane back from his contemplation.

"You've been found guilty of abusing your former authority, detective, and of helping to send at least *one* innocent man to the pen. In *my* high court, however, you won't be so lucky as to be released. The only question that remains to be answered is how you want to die."

In an attempt to buy himself more time to consider how he might change the odds that were stacking against him, Osbourne defiantly said, "I've never sent any innocent man to prison! Whether it was a mistake or no, all I do is research and file the complaint reported!"

Lane expected a similar response. "Don't fuckin' lie to me Osbourne, Roberts told me everything just before her sentence was carried out."

Osbourne's voice turned to ice, "Alright Bryant. I manipulated the statement Roberts filed! I told her what to say and helped to collect money from her family's insurance and other sources. Then I went back after you were convicted and blackmailed the bitch! That's what I do. Do you think I give a damn about you? About her? You're an idiot Bryant! I used you to blackmail her, it's a practice I've followed for years and I'm good at it!"

"Yeah. You *were* good and I *am* an idiot, but I'm an idiot with a gun to your head and an itching trigger finger." Lane stated calmly not giving in to the rage screaming in his head, in his heart! "Now tell me how you knew it was me back at the clinic."

"Like I said, you're an idiot! Von Eric, you should remember him, he informed me of Roberts' death. Said you were released a year ago and if it was you who killed Roberts then I should watch my back. It seems that you've painted yourself into a corner, Bryant! If you kill me then you'll verify Von Eric's suspicions about you but you can't let me go for fear that *I'll* verify Von Eric's suspicions about you. Although it's more likely that I'd kill you before I'd turn you in. Nobody threatens my little girls, you piece of shit!"

Osbourne was right and Lane couldn't deny it, he was in a tough situation. And he *did* threaten the girls, but that's all it was—a threat. Lane was sure that Osbourne wouldn't do anything to endanger his kids, what father would? But if Lane could use that possibility to keep the former detective under control, then it was a threat Lane would exploit. Lane's plan backfired, however. If he didn't kill Osbourne then it was very likely that he was finished. On the other hand, if Osbourne was murdered Von Eric would undoubtedly come after Lane. *Damn!* Lane thought to himself bitterly.

"Get off the highway." Lane instructed, the authority in his voice slipping away with each passing minute.

Osbourne exited as instructed. After driving aimlessly through less populated residential streets in north Houston Lane spotted a deserted ally way behind a local bar and directed Osbourne to pull and park.

After a long moment Lane said, "Tell me about Von Eric. How did he know about Roberts? Is it common for a robbery detective to get that information on a whim?"

"Von Eric hasn't been with robbery since the Roberts' case." Osbourne explained. "He transferred to homicide as soon as he could."

Curious, Lane asked, "Why would he leave such a lucrative investment as the two of you managed?"

"Von Eric?" Osbourne asked laughing. "Von Eric's a 'good' cop. He had no part in my enterprise. He left robbery because he knew I was into something, but he couldn't prove it. Try as he did, he just couldn't catch me! Still that didn't stop him from trying; I had to get one of my boys to threaten his family before he backed off. He didn't like the way I fixed Roberts' statement so he filed for a transfer that afternoon."

Lane punched Osbourne in the back of the head. "Don't fuckin' lie to me Osbourne! Von Eric was your partner, you friend I'm sure, and he's a cop! All cops have their fingers in some dirt somewhere, Von Eric is no exception. There *are* no exceptions!"

"You're wrong Bryant! Von Eric was my partner for a very short time and we were far from friends. You've watched too many movies! Von Eric's a straight cop and he's on to you Bryant, you're busted! You just don't want to admit it." Osbourne stated arrogantly. "So what do you do *now*?"

"Don't worry about me detective, I've made arrangements. I've done my research on you, just as you did on me when you helped send me to prison. Everybody knows about your cancer; which must be a painful way to die. I'm sure that you wouldn't be the first patient to consider suicide."

Osbourne's thoughts kicked into overdrive. The time had come and he was going to eat a bullet, there was no way out of it! *No* way.

"Take this and swallow!" Lane said as he handed Osbourne a small off-white pill.

Osbourne's mind came to a screeching halt. "What's this?"

"Cyanide." Lane replied bluntly. "It's fast and painless, but most importantly it will save your daughter's lives." Lane lied.

Truth be known, Lane had no idea what effects the poison would have on a person nor did he care, as long as the end result was death.

Osbourne's mind kicked back up to high gear. Did this man really believe that he would *willingly poison* himself? But didn't Bryant just say that suicide was common among terminal cancer patients? It seems that Bryant had found his way out from Von Eric's suspicions, Osbourne thought to himself as he looked at the pill in his hand. Suicide!

Looking at Lane through the rearview Osbourne recognized his own salvation as well, and possibly a little help he could use to give himself a jumpstart. "You'll let my daughters be?" Osbourne whined the question.

"Of course, now get it over with. There are others waiting for their sentencing as well." Lane's tone was icy.

Osbourne held a humbled façade. "There's something else you'll want to do." He spoke quietly.

"Make it quick detective."

"BigTime Bill Rights," Osbourne continued, "you know him? He was your judge in the case I handled."

"What about him?" Lane asked impatiently.

"He's my former business partner. The informal investigations in Detective Von Eric made the judge a very nervous man, so the son of a bitch crossed me out of a very profitable share of our business. You'll want to expose him, in order to do that you'll need his records."

Lane shook his head. "I wouldn't give a damn if the judge is exposed. He won't be alive long enough to regret any of it. Now stop wasting my time! I can still hurt your family."

Osbourne looked at the pill in his hand again; his shoulders sagged, he placed it on his tongue so that Lane could see it and made a sour expression as he chewed and swallowed it.

"There. Now will you listen to me?"

Lane nodded at the mirror, "Go ahead." Then he settled back into his seat, leveling the suppressed pistol at the back of Osbourne's seat.

"There's a floor safe under the judge's desk in his office at home. That's where he keeps all his records from our ventures as well as some portion of their profits. If you're going after him at least pull the records for somebody to find and you'll make yourself a nice little bank as well . . ."

"I don't need a nice little bank Osbourne; I have plenty of money and the means to get more, if needed." Lane spoke in an angry tone.

"Then give the cash to my kids in apology for threatening them!" Osbourne countered in a spiteful, sharp tone. "My life insurance policy is about to default."

Lane pinched the bridge of his nose between his forefinger and thumb. "Whatever Osbourne, just *die*!"

"Give me your word!" Osbourne coughed the request.

"Fine, you got it!" Lane said although he had no intention of doing *anything* that'll make his situation more complicated.

Osbourne's coughing intensified and he started convulsing. Suddenly he went rigid and his neck and back arched stiffly, then his body went limp. Osbourne fell forward smashing his head against the center of the steering wheel, sounding the horn.

"Shit!"

Lane sprang from the rear seat and grabbed at Osbourne's hair which was too short to get a hold on. The horn continued to sound loudly at the rear door to the bar where Osbourne was parked. Lane finally grabbed the man's collar, lifting his head from the horn and let him fall into the seat. Hurriedly Lane exited the sedan and fled the ally looking for a bus or a cab; something that would get him from the area quick.

Osbourne dared to smile when he heard the footfalls of his would be murderer fade into the distance. After a few more minutes the former detective sat up and retrieves his cell phone from the console. He punched in the digits and waited.

"It's Osbourne. That's right; I'm ready, only there's been a slight change. The cause of death will be suicide by cyanide." Osbourne turned the poison pill over in his hand as he spoke. "Make the adjustments and there's a large bonus for you. Now get someone over here to pick up my body. Here's the directions . . ."

* * *

"So there was no sign of a struggle?"

"That's right detective. It's suicide by poison, plain and simple."

"OK, that's all I needed to know. Thanks a lot." Von Eric hung up the phone and leaned back in his chair, looking at his partner.

"So what's on your mind, Enis?" asked Fitzgerald.

Von Eric stared intently into Fitzgerald eyes for a long moment then spoke casually. "Nothin' Norm; I was just surprised that Dave went the way he did, that's all.

"I'm gonna call it a day." Von Eric sighed as he rose to his feet and shrugged into his jacket. "My sister's expecting me in half an hour. I'm already gonna be late."

"See ya tomorrow Enis." Fitzgerald said as he watched Von Eric leave the office.

* * *

Chapter Five

AT HIS HOME in Port Arthur, Lane explained to his wife that he had some jobs to do in Austin and he would be gone for seven to ten days. When she heard the news, Carol couldn't hide the disappointment in her face and Lane recognized it immediately.

"Well baby, what do *you* think I should do? I hate being away from you and the boys for so long, but I love my job and I'm not gone as long as when I was workin' on the boats. And it pays well enough."

"You'll be gone for nearly two weeks! Again! Wasn't five years long enough, Lane?" Carol's pout tugged at the string she held on Lane's heart.

Lane sat next to her on the couch, "That was unfair Carol, but I feel the same way. When I get my next job or jobs I'll tell my boss that Austin was my last night away from home and if that's a problem then he'll have to find some one else, ok?"

Carol still didn't like the idea, but wanting to show her willingness to comprise she conceded, "Ok baby, but I need you to understand that all I want is you home at night, with me. I've lost you for so long and when you're not here, all those nights alone come back to haunt me."

"I do understand 'cause I want the same thing, but we also need the income. I'll work something out then we can go over it and if you don't like it I'll quit, ok?"

Carol stood, "No Lane, that's not ok! I don't want you to put this decision off on me. Not like that! It has to be your decision, not mine."

Lane recognized his mistake, "What I'm trying to say is if we can't 'agree' then I'll quit. Does that sound better?" He stood to face his wife as he spoke.

"No, that's not much better Lane, but I'll take what I can get. I just want . . . no, I need you here with me, ok?"

"Yeah, and I want you to be happy. More than that, I want us happy together. Ok baby?" Lane hugged his wife.

He'd bought himself ten more days under his present cover job. That might change soon if he needed more time 'out of town'.

* * *

Later that week Lane was alone in the apartment gathering his things to pack for his trip. Once finished he went to the bathroom to make one final check to be sure nothing was forgotten.

"Why do I have to hide from that . . . that *woman*?" Lane glared at himself in the mirror for a short moment. "That's my reason for living!" he replied.

After a short pause, Lane's facial expression changed. "She's nothing more than a complication! Always nagging and questioning." the hateful voice stated.

"That complication will be here long after your business in Houston is finished!" A calmer voice flowed. In regards to his wife and children, Lane's emotions reigned true and drowned out the emotions of his demon.

"Take my advice and ditch the bitch!" Lane growled at the mirror.

"No! She's my wife, not just some complication or some comparative enemy. If you can't accept that then *you* can leave!" With that final statement Lane squeezed his hand into a white knuckled fist and landed a furious blow to his temple. A painful white light flashed in Lane's vision. Then darkness . . .

. . . Laughter. Cruel, demeaning laughter. Lane opened his eyes to find himself lying on the bathroom floor.

"I've told you before, only *I* can do the things that I do. That's why I'm with you, because *you* can't. Now stop wasting time, you stupid fuck, we've got work to do and a D.A. to sentence." Lane picked himself up from the floor, grabbed his bag and headed for Houston.

* * *

Arriving in Houston, Lane followed the usual routine in purchasing his equipment. He took note that Trigga was much easier to deal with than he had been in the past. Lane's senses went on alert and stayed there until he checked into a motel, and searched all the equipment he'd received.

Something was strange with his usually defensive contact. This time Trigga seemed to be not quite as cold; friendly almost. Lane forced himself to relax once he was satisfied that no tracking devices or other such equipment had been included with his purchase.

Lane tucked his newest equipment into his travel bag and called for a taxi. "I'll be outside," Lane told the dispatcher, "The name's McGregor. Timothy McGregor."

After awhile a cab pulled into the lot that service the motel and Lane slid into the back seat.

"Where to captain?" Asked the young driver.

"Captain?" Lane asked confused. "I think you might have the wrong fare.

The driver turned around in his seat showing a large scarred and crooked nose, crooked yellowed teeth and ears that seemed to stick out at perfect ninety degree angles.

"Didn't you call for a Cab?" the driver asked.

"Sure, but I'm not a Captain," Lane stated flatly.

The driver turned back to face forward, "Well captain, if you called for a ride then I've got the right fare."

The car eased forward before Lane could shut the door. "Where to?" Lane was asked as he secured the door.

Sitting back in his seat Lane said, "How about northwest!"

The driver eyed Lane from the rearview, "Anywhere specific?" he asked.

Looking out the side window lane replied "Yeah, Willowbrook Mall."

Minutes later Lane paid the cabbie and watched him leave before he turned and walked away from the mall down FM 1960.

Full of businesses, shops, salons, bars, clubs and every type of store imaginable, 1960 was a very busy street, even for late in the afternoon near dark. Just a couple of blocks north or south of FM 1960 are residential neighborhoods but Lane stayed clear of those areas choosing instead the crowd and confusion of the busy street. Here he could blend in easily with the other pedestrians, and there are plenty of opportunities to acquire what he was looking for.

Lane strolled lazily into an Auto Zone just a couple of blocks away purchasing a small ratchet, a few sockets of various sizes and a flat head screw driver. Afterwards it didn't take long for Lane to find the truck he was searching for, colored in a very common blue and grey. Satisfied that there were no distinguishing appearances which might separate it from other pick-ups of the same make and model, Lane took the front license plate from the vehicle, tucking it under his jacket.

Nearly an hour later, Lane found himself walking through a parking lot which served a movie theater and a wide array of shops, café's, clothing stores and the like. Continuing his search, Lane found another truck of the exact likeness to the first with no distinguishing factors other than the license plates. The VIN would be the only way to tell the difference from this truck and the other once Lane changed the plates.

Taking both plates from the previous pick-up would have set off an alarm, however, people generally never notice the plates missing from the front of any vehicle. And although it's a law in Texas to have both plates mounted, it is very rarely enforced. The tags that were posted to the plates in times past now were posted on the inside windshield of the vehicles in Texas, making the front plate identical to the rear plates.

Lane retrieved the flat-head screw driver from his pocket, climbed into the bed of the Chevy Silverado and fitted the tool between the sliding rear windows. Once the tool would enter no further, Lane gave the handle a solid hit with the palm of his hand shattering the locking mechanism but preserving the glass. After a quick scan of the lot Lane squeezed through the open window, shutting the glass behind him.

Moving fast and efficiently, Lane retrieved the tire tool from its case under the rear seat then climbed into the driver's seat. He used the tool to pound on the left side of the steering column, destroying the plastic casing and exposing the mechanics of the ignition. A toothed bar ran the length of the column secured in place by a solid plastic ring fastened to the back side of the ignition switch.

Lane used the screw driver to pop that plastic ring off then placed the flat of the screw driver between the teeth of the sliding bar, pushing it toward himself and starting the engine. Quickly he left the area in the stolen truck, stopping a few blocks away to replace the rear license plate with the one he'd taken off the first truck and removing the front plate altogether. Lane returned to his motel room satisfied that the truck would not be discovered.

He took a few minutes to change his clothes and freshen up, washing his face and hands. Energized by the fact that nothing had gone astray so far, Lane began to feel his confidence returning. After the shocking news he received from the late Dave Osbourne about Von Eric being on to him, he was starting to doubt his ability to complete his task. Now he was full of renewed vigor.

He tucked his equipment under the front seat and drove to the nearest supply store. Anxious to reach his destination Lane practically ran through the large store gathering the few extra supplies which he thought he needed. A sixteen-ounce ball-ping hammer, twenty-five feet of nylon rope and a pair of medium sized bolt cutters.

* * *

Driving south toward Fort Bend just outside of Houston, Lane's confidence swayed. As he neared the residence of Keith LeGross he began to doubt once again.

"What is it now?" Lane screamed at the pitiful expression of worry facing him from the mirror.

"Well? Do you have something to say? If you do then spit it out, if not then go the fuck away and let me handle this."

A softer voice responded, "If you kill a District Attorney, they'll never stop looking for me."

"Let them look! How a pussy like you ever survived the pen is beyond me. Those people stole something from me, from us, that can't be replaced and I intend to take something from them as well." Lane violently punched the dash board, cracking the plastic, "Understand? They have to pay!"

Another blow broke the plastic, the jagged shards cut into Lane's knuckles, "The have to die!"

Another blow bloodied his hand further but that only fueled Lane's rage. Slamming his bloodied fist repeatedly into the dash, no longer feeling the pain Lane chanted, "They have to die!" Emphasizing the word 'die' with each blow.

The rage played out leaving Lane's hand throbbing and bloody. He pulled into a Walgreens and searched the cab of the truck for a first aid kit then cleaned and bandaged his wound. He bought some mild pain killers and bottled water before he resumed his drive to the LeGross residence.

District Attorney Keith LeGross' two story brick home was located in an expensive neighborhood on the north side of Fort Bend County. Lane parked the stolen truck next to a pay phone located near the side walk of a strip mall across the busy street from LeGross' neighborhood. Standing at the phone, handset held to his ear, Lane studied the armed security of the community and tried to locate any security cameras.

The loud, insistent beeping emanating from the handset snapped Lane from his obsessive observation. After replacing the handset Lane turned toward the truck he'd been driving then froze in mid stride. Sitting in a hunter green Buick Park Avenue, was Harris County's youngest ever District Attorney. With both hands on the steering wheel he eyed the Boulevard for a break in traffic that he could maneuver into. Lane stood staring at the man until he steered the vehicle out of the mall lot and into the flow of traffic.

Lane, a violent surge of energy coursing through him, ran to the stolen truck and pursued the D.A., recklessly veering in and out of traffic. Nearing the Buick, Lane reigned in his impulses to fall in behind his target, following him carefully and cautiously.

* * *

The Montrose area of Houston is notorious for harboring activities that are frowned on by most of today's society. Gay prostitution with a variety of clubs and bars that would suit the tastes and desires of even the most twisted of depravities. The latter of these less desirable vices seemed, to Lane, to be Keith LeGross' preference.

Lane casually passed LeGross' car as it entered the lot of a spa/club whose cheap sign proclaimed its name, "Sadist 14480." Underlying the buildings title a statement read "Welcome to Sadistic Sunday @ Sadist!" A funny statement for Thursday night, Lane thought as he continued past the establishment.

After a few blocks, Lane negotiated a U-Turn returning to a vacant lot on the opposite side of the street. The lot serviced a novelty sex shop, located at the far corner from the club where the Buick had parked. The view from Lane's position was unobstructed and he could clearly see the rear door of the club. The D.A. was speaking with a young shirtless man who played with the hair at the back of LeGross' head with one hand while his other accepted what appeared to be a wad of cash. Lane watched the shirtless man slide his empty hand down the front of LeGross' shirt, grab the D.A. by the top of his pants and lead him through the entrance.

"I wish I had a camera," Lane said considering the humiliation that could be placed on the officials of Harris County should this encounter be publicized. That humiliation would prove to be a huge black eye to Houston's judicial employees and could possibly draw some eyes to the unjust and illegal proceedings within the county's judicial system.

He retrieved the nap sack from under the seat, withdrawing the suppressed Walther P22 pistol and a hand held tazer stun gun. He counted out ten one hundred dollar bills to cover the cost of information, if needed. Then pocketing the cash and tazer and fitting the .22 pistol in the waist of his jeans, Lane exited the truck and hurried across to the club.

* * *

Lane surveyed the exterior of the building as he approached. Just inside the front glass door stood a bulky door man who seemed more concerned with the buttons on his cell phone than who might want to pass by his post. Focused on the solid door near the rear of the club where LeGross entered, Lane avoided the front door by ducking in behind the few vehicles parked in the lot.

He made his way to the unmanned door unnoticed but just as he arrived the door swung open and a young man wearing a lot of makeup stepped out and looked at Lane, "This is the V.I.P. entrance honey, you'll have to use the front door."

"Oh. I'm sorry." Lane apologized.

The young man looked to Lane curiously. "You're new here aren't you?"

'Shit' Lane thought to himself, alarms sounding in his head. "Yeah, that's right." He answered.

"Well just talk to Teddy Bear at the front door. Tell him that Katy said for you to check about the V.I.P. rooms." The young prostitute lit a cigarette as he spoke.

Lane couldn't risk being identified by the doorman *or* this clown. He didn't want to kill the guy but couldn't see any way to avoid it aside from walking away, and that simply wasn't an option.

Lane reached to the small caliber pistol at the small of his back. "Hey buddy, ya got another smoke?"

"Sure thing sweetie." The prostitute replied as he reached into the thigh pocket of his army fatigues.

As soon as the man lowered his eyes, Lane brought the pistol around and placed a suppressed round into the guy's head. The Sadist employee crumbled silently to the ground. Lane grabbed him by his arms and dragged him quickly to the far corner of the lot behind the building, placing the body next to a large dumpster where it couldn't easily be seen.

"Sorry weirdo, you're just collateral; nothing personal." Lane mumbled as he dropped the corpse.

Quiet and clean, Lane had taken the life of a complete stranger with the efficiency of a trained assassin, and for no other reason than to gain access to his real target. The realization of this truth and the implications of what it meant echoed through Lane's thoughts as he inspected the area for possible indications of what just transpired.

Lane congratulated himself on his choice of weapon, acknowledging the effectiveness of the P22 without the mess which would be produced by so many of the larger guns. That is until he realized that he only had nine rounds left. Lane now cursed himself, making a mental note to buy at least one extra clip the next time he purchased a weapon.

Back at the 'V.I.P.' entrance, Lane steadied himself for what might lay inside this den of decadence. Holding his breath he entered through the door as quietly as possible, finding himself on the top landing of a concrete stairwell that descended one flight. Following the stairs, Lane held his weapon slightly behind his right leg at his side.

The base of the stairs were located at the intersection of two halls, one leading to the right and one heading straight ahead. Lane descended slowly listening intently for any sound louder than the muffled techno-rave music that permeated through the ceiling from the club above. Hearing voices from a distance down the hall to the right, Lane froze. He cautiously descended the last few steps and listened intently but was unable to make out what was being discussed.

Carefully he peeked around the corner to see the young shirtless prostitute who LeGross entered the club with. He stood, clad in a hot pink thong and matching high-heel pumps. The prostitute shoved some cash into the hands of a huge biker looking giant who glanced at the bills then produced a small bag. For a short moment Lane found himself wondering what had happened in this kid's life to make him so fucked-up now.

He watched as the pair entered different doors that were placed a fair distance apart along the same wall. Lane could only guess, but he was sure the giant biker would be able to see every thing that was happening in the next room. He ran down the hall to the door which the biker entered and, leaning on the wall next to the door, he checked the knob. Unlocked, Lane eased into the room, quietly shutting it behind himself. The biker, unaware, was fumbling with a camcorder mounted atop a tripod, obviously focused to record the activity in the next room.

This room was heavily padded for sound proofing and designed for both surveillance and security, evidenced by a two-way mirror mounted into the wall where the video-cam was set up. The floor had been cheaply carpeted and the sparse furniture seemed to have been picked from trash discarded by its previous owners. The only light in the room emanated from a ceramic lamp, which was placed on an unstable stand, in the corner near the door.

Glancing through the glass at which the video-cam was pointing, Lane could see the male prostitute receiving oral sex from LeGross, who had been tethered to some form of futon. Lane slid the deadbolt into place causing an audible 'click' to sound through the room. The biker fumbling with the camera looked to see Lane leveling his pistol toward him, and straightened raising his hands.

"I hope you're recording that sick shit!" Lane stated flatly.

As soon as the words escaped his lips a large forearm crashed down into his wrist. Lane reflexively squeezed the trigger, firing off a round with a 'spith'. The stray round impacted the biker's knee, bringing the large man to the floor growling in pain. Lane hadn't noticed though, a ferocious blow caused a white veil to flash behind his eyes and sent him sprawling onto the floor.

His vision swam in and out of focus, but he managed to pull himself to his knees, feeling blindly around the carpet for his dropped pistol. The lamp, arching in a downward swing, smashed into the back of his head, knocked him back to the floor. After a moment he felt himself being lifted into the air, then felt the breath forced from his lung when he was slammed to the floor on his back.

Gasping for the air that had been stolen from him, Lane searched his jacket pocked for the tazer he'd brought with him. The monster that now stood over him kicked him hard in the ribs. "What's this here? Some kind of badass or somethin'?!" The biker looked at his partner who still grasped his shattered knee, "Or some fairy's jealous lover?"

"You alright, Doc?" The biker asked, receiving a quick nod from the injured man.

The biker returned his attention to Lane, who had finally been able to choke down some air.

"We can't allow this type of shit to go on in our club, can we Doc?" The big man said, then he back handed Lane across the cheek.

The man kneeled over Lane, one hand grasped around Lane's throat restricting his breath.

"You think you can just waltz on in here and run the joint!" The statement was followed by an open handed slap. "Well I've got news for you punk! You're one dead fairy!"

The man landed another open hand across Lane's face then he tightened both hands around Lane's throat. Desperate, Lane continued his fruitless search for the pistol that had been knocked from his grasp. Seconds passed as his right hand ran across the carpet hoping to find something, *anything* that would get this beast off him and his left hand searched frantically for the tazer in his pocket. His vision darkened steadily as the seconds ticked away.

Lane's wits were failing fast. He felt something in his right hand, not knowing what it was or how it got there. Then, in a miraculous flash of insight, Lane understood exactly *'everything'*. He withdrew the tazer from his pocket as he swung a vicious right hand at his attacker. That hand drove a wickedly jagged ceramic shard deep into his attacker's neck.

The monstrous biker released his hold on Lane, who was ready with his tazer. As soon as he was released Lane jerked the shard from his attacker, causing a line of blood to spurt from the gash in short intervals, then pressed his alternate weapon into the groin of the biker and fired. The man toppled from atop Lane, unconscious from the tazer and bleeding profusely from the wound in his neck. Seeing his partner fall unconscious, 'Doc' scurried across the carpet, dragging his ruined knee. Lane coughed and gasped down fresh air in huge swallows, then nearly vomited as he pulled himself to his hands and knees.

Just as he'd gotten himself under control he saw 'Doc' for the first time since he'd been attacked. Just behind Lane, the biker made his way toward the pistol Lane had lost. Moving as fast as he could, Lane spun around to block the hand that now held his gun from coming to bear on him. In that instant Lane attacked with the tazer, sending the biker into a spasmic frenzy which caused him to fire a round harmlessly into the sound proofed wall. 'Doc' fell flat to the floor, dropping the pistol.

Lane stood on an unstable floor, his knees wobbling and weak, coughed down more air into his lungs then noticed 'Doc' slowly pulling himself backward, away from Lane. The injured man screamed in agony when Lane stomped on his damaged knee.

"Playtime's over tough guy", Lane said wearily then fired two rounds into the man's head.

* * *

Lane set himself on the edge of a cheap stool near the far wall from the door, replaying the scene slowly in his head. Then he went to work removing any traces of himself. As he was picking up the ceramic shards of the lamp he'd been hit with, he spotted LeGross, who was now allowing his much younger mate to sodomize him. Lane ran to the video camcorder. The screen which stemmed out the side at a right angle revealed the 'rec' light in the lower left corner, indicating that the scene beyond the wall was in fact being filmed.

"You're one sick bastard, LeGross. Now the world's gonna know what a twisted fuck you are!"

Lane finished his clean-up then checked on LeGross again. The D.A. was alone in the room, dressing himself. Lane ejected the disk from the camcorder wiping the surface afterward. Locking the doorknob and wiping away his prints he hurried from the building as cautiously as possible.

* * *

Lane made it back to the stolen truck without any more encounters and his head pounded in pain as he climbed into the cab.

"What the hell do you think you're doin'?" He growled to himself as he cranked the engine.

"I've got that twisted shit on disk and that's enough to kill his career. He'll probably kill himself . . ." An opened hand slapped Lane hard across the cheek.

"The hell he will, that's *my* job! He's still got a sentence to face and he'll pay what he owes just like we had to!"

Lane drove the truck back to the club and waited for LeGross to exit. He was standing in the shadows behind the stolen truck on the far side of the lot when LeGross made his exit. Walking briskly, but quietly across the blacktop, Lane came within tazer range as the D.A. turned off the alarm in his Buick using the remote. Tazering LeGross at the base of his skull just as he reached to open the driver's door he knocked the man to the ground.

"Oh my god!" came a nearly whispered voice from behind Lane. Without thinking, operating solely on survival instincts that were heightened by the previous assault, Lane dropped the tazer to the ground. In one smooth, fluid motion he spun, dropping to one knee and bringing the suppressed pistol from his waist band, firing three rounds as fast as he could pull the trigger.

The male prostitute which LeGross has been having sex with was now dressed in a mini-skirt and matching blouse and stood grasping his throat. The young man must have put on some type of custom bra, because his once flat chest now boasted a pair of full breasts. Lane was amazed at the transformed man standing before him in heels and a wig. The illusion was so complete Lane initially thought he'd shot a teenage girl.

The first bullet fired had hit the wall of the club low and to Lane's right, the second, however, struck the transvestite in the center of the neck. The third round had leveled with the second but was wide to Lane's left, again hitting the clubs exterior wall.

Lane rose from his knee, ran to the prostitute and whispered, "Sorry Kid, but you're a liability."

Lane took a step back and fired one more round into the prostitute's head. He was lifting the still unconscious District Attorney off the ground before the prostitute fell to it. Lane carried the man to the cab of the Chevy and set him onto the floor board, then bound his hand and feet with nylon rope. After binding his prisoner, Lane hurriedly left the area expecting to see red and blue lights flash behind him at any moment.

Maintaining the speed limit on the highway proved to be more of a challenge than Lane had thought. Control reigned within Lane's members but anxiousness was threatening to rend that control from him. He seemed to spend as much time studying his rear views as he spent studying the road ahead.

LeGross was tied and cramped into the small space on the floor board between the seat and dash. In a hushed, whimpered tone he pleadingly asked "Why are you doing this?"

The question went unanswered for several long minutes. When LeGross asked again Lane simply looked at the pathetic man, veered the truck to the shoulder of the highway, placed the vehicle in park and engaged the hazard lights.

After Lane had violently stomped LeGross' head a few times, he warned the D.A., "You make another fucking sound and I'll use your severed dick to gag you with!"

LeGross didn't ask any more questions, but after a few minutes Lane could smell the strong odor of urine that had saturated LeGross' pants.

A short while later Lane entered an abandoned warehouse compound on the East side of Houston, located near a popular beer distribution center. Lane used the bolt cutters to let himself into the compound and proceeded to the furthest building. Having gained access to an empty warehouse, Lane drove the truck in and closed the large door.

From an interior office, Lane retrieved a large wooden chair and placed it in the center of the empty building before returning to the truck to bring his prisoner out. LeGross was struggling to free himself from his bonds when the passenger door opened. Glaring at his prisoner with a evil grin spreading across his face, Lane pressed a button on the seat causing it to regress slowly away from LeGross.

"What do you want with me?" LeGross ask pleadingly.

Lane simply held his menacing glare allowing his grin to fade into a malevolent snarl. When the seat had fully regressed Lane grabbed the rope that bound LeGross' feet as though he might release the binds. Instead he jerked LeGross from the cab of the truck causing the D.A. to hit the concrete hard, knocking the breath from his lungs. Lane then dragged LeGross to the large chair and secured him to it using the last of the nylon rope.

Again LeGross whined, "What do you want?"

In response to the repeated question, Lane landed a solid fist into the D.A.'s nose. With a resounding 'pop', the nose laid over to one side, bleeding profusely.

"Shut up!" Lane said calmly.

Returning to the stolen truck, Lane lowered the tail-gate and laid out each piece of equipment, holding the items up for his hostage to see before placing them neatly side by side; the DVD of LeGross and his lover, the suppressed P22, the tazer, a sixteen ounce ball-ping hammer, bolt cutters, a 9mm Berretta and an empty forty ounce beer bottle. Humming quietly as he retrieved the tools he bought earlier Lane crawled under the truck. LeGross strained to see what his captor was working on, but to no avail. After a short moment, Lane pulled himself from underneath the truck, placed the beer bottle on the floor and ran a short black hose into it. Turning on the ignition, Lane allowed the Chevy's electronic fuel pump fill the bottle with gasoline then reconnected the hose. He returned to the rear of the truck with the bottle of gas and perched himself on the edge of the tailgate.

"Well Mr. Keith LeGross, it seems you've been caught a little out of your forum. That's a *very* dangerous place to be . . ."

"Why are you doing this?" LeGross interrupted half screaming, half crying.

Enraged, Lane grabbed up his 9mm. In a flash he was upon LeGross, landing a vicious blow with the butt of the weapon. The following blow cut a deep gash into LeGross' cheek, fracturing the bone.

"*DO NOT* interrupt me again, Mr. District Attorney! You're in my world now" Lane growled maliciously.

He tucked the pistol into his waist band and began pacing back and forth in front of his captive.

"Court is now in session. I am the witness, the prosecutor, the judge," Lane stopped in front of LeGross glaring, "and the executioner."

Wanting to plead with his captor, but fearful of another beating LeGross only shook his head. Tears streamed down his cheek mixing with his blood, giving the appearance that he was 'crying' blood.

Lane continued his pacing. "You're probable wondering who I am, but before I tell you that, I will explain *why* I'm doing this.

"Several years ago you prosecuted me for a crime that I didn't commit. I pleaded with you and the court, much like you're pleading with me now, trying to explain that it wasn't me. I was ignored by my attorney, you and the judge. Nobody would listen to my claims and as a result I lost several years of my life. That time cannot be given back to me.

"You and your people sent me to prison under the guise of justice. Now I'm free and *I* want justice! I want justice for the *injustice* that you willingly took part in. I want *my* justice," Lane shook his head as he spoke, laughing at the irony. "*Criminal* justice."

Lane retrieved the ball-ping hammer from the truck holding the end of the handle between thumb and fore finger, swinging the hanging head in the motion of a pendulum.

Lane stated flatly, "I'm tired of this shit. Tell me about Detective Osbourne."

"I don't know a Detective Osbourne." LeGross whined.

Lane shook his head making a "tck, tck" sound between his teeth. He sat Indian style in front of LeGross, placed the hammer to the side and removed the D.A.'s shoes and socks. He placed the items in LeGross' lap and picked up the hammer once more.

"Do you like movies Mr. LeGross?" Lane asked in a calm tone.

LeGross looked puzzled, wondering what that had to do with any this.

Lane smiled, "I love movies. I love music too, but for now I want to talk about movies. Have you ever seen the Mel Gibson film 'Pay Back'?"

Confused, LeGross shook his head.

"In the movie, Mel Gibson's character was tied barefoot to a chair. He was asked a question and when he didn't answer . . ." *Clank*.

The sound echoed throughout the empty warehouse followed by LeGross tormented screams.

"Tell me about Osbourne!" Lane demanded.

CLANK!

More screaming.

"That's only one toe LeGross. You have nine more and ten fingers. Tell me what you know!"

"I don't know anything about Osbourne!" LeGross cried blindly.

Clank!

More screaming.

"You're running out of toes. Tell me what you *do* know about."

LeGross began explaining the ties that he shared with several other city officials including 'Big Time' Bill Rights, Lane's judge. He explained, as best he could, how those 'ties' connected to a local white supremist organization. Or more accurately put *the* white supremist organization. LeGross explained how the organization, called the Texas Aryan Coalition, gained several acquisitions including the club LeGross frequented in Montrose. Lane felt a pang in his gut at the discovery that he may have killed some of the members of Houston's most powerful Nazi affiliation.

Shaking off the distraction Lane asked, "What does *that* have to do with sending *me* to the pen?"

LeGross explained that members of the Coalition were cut a lot of slack in court when they got busted for something.

"In return, those of us who play ball reap certain rewards."

Lane just gained confirmation of Osbourne's claim about Judge Rights being dirty, but he didn't really care about any of that at the moment.

"You still haven't answered my question. What does that have to do with *me*?" Lane interrupted wearily.

"We have to protect our careers." LeGross said flatly, "We can't let too many people off the hook. We have to secure a certain number of convictions in order to insure our positions and to do that we have to make some . . . sacrifices."

There it was, plain and simple. It all boiled down to money and power. From LeGross and Rights, to Osbourne and Roberts, to God knew who else. How many other 'gangs' have worked out this same deal, or is there only one. God *damn* politicians!

"Very good Mr. District Attorney, you were very convincing. Now why don't you tell me about Detective Osbourne?" Lane asked rising to his feet.

"I told you, I don't know the man."

"And I've made it clear that I know you're lying." Lane returned the hammer to the truck and retrieved the bolt cutters.

"The man is a highly decorated officer of the H.P.D. and he's been in the papers and on T.V. several times. He is now the *late* former Detective Dave Osbourne."

Lane stood next to his captive holding his left thumb with the bolt cutters.

LeGross shook his head vigorously, begging Lane, "No! Please I've never met him. I've only heard rum . . ."

LeGross' pleas turned into screams as Lane snipped his thumb from its place.

"That's for lying to me LeGross. Don't let it happen again". Lane walked around the chair to clasp the right thumb with the bolt cutters then waited for LeGross' cries to quiet some.

"Tell me LeGross!" Lane demanded.

Through grunts and sobs LeGross explained how several officers in the police and sheriffs departments would bribe or scare witnesses into making statements that would ultimately help secure convictions in court.

"Osbourne got greedy. He brought too many investigations on himself and made the coalition nervous. It fell on Rights to take care of the situation but instead of eliminating Osbourne, Right forced him to retire."

"Ok. That makes sense. I believe you, LeGross." Lane spoke pleasantly, releasing the D.A.'s thumb. "Now tell me about Osbourne's partner, Detective Von Eric." Lane's instruction was a quiet one.

LeGross had just relaxed a bit, thinking that his cooperation had bought his freedom. When he was asked about Von Eric, his eyes grew wide. He knew what would follow.

"Please! He's nobody. A . . . A do-gooder."

"Bullshit!" Lane screamed furiously then gripped LeGross' thumb again and snipped it off.

Raising his voice above his captive's screams Lane continue, "Von Eric's a cop! All cops have their hand in some dirt somewhere. Tell me where Von Eric's hands are".

"He . . . good . . . clean . . ." LeGross couldn't form his sentences coherently.

"No!" Lane yelled. "I'll hear if before I leave here!" Lane snipped off another of LeGross' fingers.

"Should I sever all your fingers?" Lane continued to yell above LeGross' screams. "Maybe I'll cut off your balls! Tell me what I want to hear LeGross, and I make it all go away!" Lane continued his yelling even after LeGross' screams fell into whimpers and sobs.

"No? Fine!" Lane tossed the bolt cutters onto the tailgate.

Holding up the DVD disk so that LeGross could see it Lane asked "See this? This is a recording of the latest fling you've had with your boyfriend. I'll be e-mailing a copy of this to every news network in the country.

"I only had to kill two bikers who beat the shit out of me. Not to mention some fag, oh and your boyfriend too. Sorry about that but I couldn't have him identifying me. Besides, I hate fags nearly as much as I hate cops . . . and lawyers."

Setting the disc back in its place, Lane grabbed the bottle of gasoline then stood before LeGross, who seemed to be teetering on the edge of unconsciousness. Lane splashed the gasoline into LeGross' face.

"Wake up Counselor. You don't have much time left. I'd like to go over one more thing with you and it looks like you're loosing quite a bit of blood, though I'm no doctor. I'd hate for you to bleed to death. No, I couldn't allow that."

LeGross' vision swam into focus, centering on his captor. The last words spoken caught his attention; again he dared to hope he might survive the ordeal, until he heard the next few words.

"That's right Keith", Lane teased," bleeding to death would be too easy for you. Too . . . *peaceful*." Splashing more of the gasoline onto LeGross as he spoke, Lane took careful notice of the horrified expression in LeGross' face. Soon the D.A.'s clothes were saturated with the flammable fluid, burning his skin. Lane set the empty bottle in the bed of the truck then, lighting a cigarette, turned to face LeGross.

"I sentence you to die for the crimes you've committed against me and others like me. Good bye LeGross and good riddance."

Lane took a long drag from the smoke then thumped it onto LeGross' lap. The sound of the fuel's ignition resounded thunderously throughout the empty warehouse, but was quickly drowned out be LeGross' screams. Pleading for his life or to end it, Lane couldn't be sure, LeGross fought against his restraints which seemed to be holding up better than their prisoner.

Lane grinned at the spectacle, "You helped to steal five years from me, Keith LeGross. Time which is not returnable, therefore this court has sentenced you to death and your personal affairs to be known nation wide by the publication of exhibit A," Lane held up the DVD disk, "So it has been ordered, so let it be done!" He had to yell above the screams of his prisoner.

Lane began to go over his steps covering all traces that could be led back to him. The building began to fill with smoke and the stench of burning flesh. He was eager to leave, but wasn't entirely sure LeGross had been killed by the fire even after he had stopped screaming and squirming. Not wanting to touch the charred flesh in order to check for a pulse, Lane stared and the unmoving lump of burnt meat for a long while.

Finally he pulled the 9mm from his waist and fired three rounds into LeGross' chest, making it apparent that the same person who killed Roberts also killed the District Attorney. It was a warning for those who framed him. The fact that the police might figure him as a suspect was an unwanted risk but Lane didn't consider that. He wanted the others, like Bill Rights, to know he was coming. When this body is found, they'll know . . . they'll all know!

"Well like I said, 'I'm no doctor', but I do believe that'll do it." Lane was speaking more to LeGross' corpse than to himself.

"Good Bye, LeGross!"

Lane returned to his hotel room to clean himself up, disposing of his equipment in his typical manner—dropping it all into the inter-coastal canal near the Port of Houston. Afterward, Lane drove the stolen truck to a river a couple of miles away on I-10 East in an area called Channel View then walked back to the hotel to clean up, grab his belongings and his own Chevy truck without bothering to check-out. Returning to the stolen truck parked near the asphalt boat ramp at the rivers' edge, Lane poured five gallons of gasoline all over the vehicle. He set the fire, which caused the truck to explode shortly after he left and hurried east bound down I-10 back to Beaumont then home to Port Arthur leaving the river far behind. The River's name . . . Lost.

* * *

"My God! Baby what happened to you? Are you ok?" The sight of Carol nearly broke Lane's heart. Just for an instant he wanted to tell her everything. The turmoil raging within him seemed to be overwhelming. But for him to ever speak of any of the things he's done or that he'd planned to do, even to his wife, would be to seal his own death. Carol had a good soul and even her love for Lane wouldn't keep her from turning him in, thinking that he needed psychiatric help. Lane thought to himself, Carol just wouldn't understand.

"No baby, I'm not ok. I hurt like hell and I'm lucky to be walking after the fall I took. Two stories face first off the roof of one of my jobs. I just want to lie down and whimper for awhile, ok." Lane kissed his wife, wrapping his arms around her petite frame. "I'll fill you in on the details when I get up, ok?"

"But you could have a concussion. You shouldn't go to sleep like that." Carol's concern brought a smile to Lane's face.

"I'll be fine. I stayed on the job a few hours with the owner of the place then made the drive home with no problems. I'm ok, baby. Besides, I had a talk with the boss today and I want to get your input on the subject, ok?"

"Alright Lane" Carol said at length. "Go get some rest it looks like you need it."

Lane turned to leave the room but Carol grabbed his arm, turning him around to face her again then kissed him tenderly on his swollen lips. "I Love you."

"I Love you, too!" Lane responded sincerely then went off to bed.

* * *

Chapter Six

JUDGE 'BIG TIME' Bill Rights sat in his home office with a phone to his ear. He listened half-heartedly to the person on the other end as he chewed two aspirin into chalky powder and chased them down with a three finger pour of bourbon; his third that morning.

"Are you with me Bill?" The distant voice asked, bringing Rights back into the conversation.

"Yeah J.T. I hear you. So far we don't have any leads and there's no sign of the District Attorney." Rights fingered his empty glass trying to block out the pounding in his head.

"I don't give a spit about LeGross, Bill! I want the man who killed my guys at the club. I don't want him *arrested* either!" The smooth voice that came from the phone was full of assurance. "We'll take care of him on our end. I just need you to identify him. Understood?" A short pause, "Who's working the case?"

Rights hesitated just a moment, "Detectives Fitzgerald and Von Eric are at the scene now."

Rights dreaded the question that was sure to follow. There was no easy way to answer it. Hearing the unwelcomed question come to his ears, Rights released his held breath with an audible sigh.

"Do we have them in our pocket?" J.T. demanded a second time, knowing the answer from Rights hesitance.

"No sir." Rights responded weakly.

In an instant, J.T.'s smooth, assured voice became strained; controlled. "Get them in our pocket Bill! Or get one of our guys in their position. I don't care which and I don't care how.

Rights rested his forehead in the palm of his hand. He couldn't say anything. He couldn't tell J.T. that it wasn't possible. That may turn out to be a fatal mistake. Yet he couldn't replace the team, and they wouldn't be bought.

"Make it happen and get back to me." J.T. ordered and calmly terminated the call.

Removing his feet from atop of the expensive desk that served as the center piece to his exquisitely furnished office, J.T. rose from his seat.

Pressing the intercom button to summon his secretary he politely asked, "Jill could you see me in my office, please?"

"Yes sir, Mr. White." responded the sensual voice from the phones speaker.

Stepping around his desk, J.T. stood in the middle of his office awaiting his aide. A moment later a soft knock issued from the door as it quietly swung inward.

"You need me, sir?" Jill asked innocently.

"Yes Jill." White spoke softly as he approached his young secretary. "I'll need you to take a dictation."

Just as the words left his lips, White grabbed Jill's lustrous blond hair violently pulling her head back and exposing her throat. He then slammed her against the door she just entered, deriving from her first a grunt, then a sigh of arousal. Shoving his free hand into the woman's blouse, White roughly groped her ample breasts.

"Take *this* dictation, you fuckin' whore!" He growled, pulling Jill hard by her hair until she was on her knees.

Unzipping the front of White's pants Jill freed his erect member, only then was she released. Jill took her employer full into her mouth, drawing and animalistic growl of desire from him. She was proud of her talents and her charms and didn't mind performing them for the much older man. After all if it wasn't for him, she'd probably still be fighting off the drunken aggressors back at the cabaret where White found her.

After a few short minutes, Jill had devoured what White had given her, with an erotically wicked smile. She felt herself being pulled by her hair once again; it was ok though she liked it rough. White stood her to her feet, spun her away from him and pressed her face into the solid door.

Violently groping her breast again with his free hand, he whispered into her ear, "That was real good, Jill. Why don't you get cleaned up and I'll buy you lunch."

Jill reached behind her to fondle White's erection, "But sir, I just had lunch." She said devilishly.

As though he hadn't heard her, White continued, "Then maybe we'll drive to Galveston Island and I'll show you the new bag of toys I bought especially for you."

"I'd like that." Jill responded in the sexiest bedroom tone she could muster.

White backed away a few steps, zipping himself up while Jill straightened her clothes and hair then turned to leave.

"Uh . . . Jill." White stopped her.

She looked back to see him pointing a spot on his cheek. Reaching up to wipe her own cheek with a finger, she found a small drop of semen, which she enticingly licked away.

"Thank you, Mr. Mayor." She said then left the office.

* * *

"Christ, what a mess." Detective Fitzgerald sighed, standing in the basement of Sadist 14480.

"That it is Norm." Von Eric commented as he examined the two bullet wounds in one of the biker's head.

Looking at his partner with concern filling his eyes, Von Eric asked, "This is the second body at the club that fits your 'execution style' murder. Could there be a connection to the Roberts killings?"

Fitzgerald glanced at his younger partner thoughtfully. After a long moment he finally shook his head. "I don't think so Enis. I wouldn't bet that a biker and the prostitute would be considered targets worthy of that type of assassination. Again, I'd bet that the D.A. was the target and things got out of hand. Look here." Fitzgerald pointed to the camcorder. "It's empty. I'd say that there's some pretty interesting activity burned on the disk that was in here."

Von Eric inspected the open camcorder. "Do you think LeGross could've been involved in that activity or do you think he was the one filming it?"

"I don't have a clue. We'll find out when the finger-prints come back. This much I *do* know—if LeGross was in there," Fitzgerald indication the room opposite the recorder, "Then Harris County is headed for a huge embarrassment."

"I don't think we should rule out abduction" Von Eric cut in.

"Oh, I think you're right. LeGross will turn up but I don't think he'll be in any condition to give us any answers." The senior detective exited the room as he spoke, leaving Von Eric alone.

Keith LeGross, Von Eric thought cynically, what was this about? His thoughts drifted to Bryant again, wasn't LeGross the prosecutor in that case? The detective wasn't sure but he vowed to check into it. Maybe he should make a trip to Port Arthur and see Bryant for himself. But what if Bryant was clean, then what?

Again Von Eric remembered how healthy former Detective Osbourne seemed to be, especially for someone who'd gone through repeated chemotherapy treatments. The man obviously killed his doctor, but committing suicide didn't seem like something the bullheaded detective would do. Too many things didn't add up Von Eric decided. Something was amiss and it was definitely bigger than an ex-con like Bryant. Whether Bryant was involved or not, he still needed to be questioned, if for no other reason than to settle Von Eric's suspicions.

"Hey Enis!" Fitzgerald's voice pulled Von Eric from his contemplation. "We've got another one. Took one to the head, you need to check it out so they can move the body."

"Alright Norm, let's go have a look." Von Eric sighed, distraught about where his thoughts seem to be leading him.

* * *

Chapter Seven

OUTSIDE LANE BRYANT'S apartment the misty predawn fog sat heavily in the parking lot. A lone figure stood in the shadows watching as Bryant, dressed in jogging pants and a light shirt, performed some stretching exercises then took off at a trot. The fog wrapped itself around Bryant's exit and suppressed his foot falls into silence. The dense figure stepped out from his concealment and approached the blue and grey Silverado. The fog seemed to lift a little revealing the face of Dave Osbourne, his hair matted to his head from the misty fog. Osbourne was amazed that Bryant still drove the same truck and lived in the same apartment after five years in prison and began to doubt the truth of it until he'd seen Bryant come out of his apartment.

At the cab of the truck, Osbourne raised short the antenna on a small black box he carried with him. A red led light began blinking slowly when he flipped the switch up. Then he reached as far as he could down between the trucks cab and bed, attaching the box by its powerful magnet. Osbourne watched the screen on another hand held device as he walked back the way he came. Soon but not just yet Bryant, he thought to himself smiling, you've still got some work to do for me. Then Osbourne's figure disappeared into the fog.

Bryant returned from his jog to the corner store. He then cooked breakfast, as was his custom, woke his family then hit the shower while they ate. Afterward he sat at the table to read the newspaper while his family prepared themselves for the day ahead.

He was relieved to discover that there were no leads in the investigation of the multiple murders in Houston's Montrose area the week before. Harris County District Attorney, Keith LeGross, whose car was found at the scene, was still missing and presumed dead. Questions had risen about his possible participation in the murders until disturbing video footage was delivered via E-Mail from an unknown source. The footage revealed the Harris County D.A. participating in several extreme acts of a homosexual nature. The consensus of the local authorities was that if the now former District Attorney had in fact been involved with the murders, this tape of him would not have been allowed to surface. Lane's smile broadened across his face. He made a mental note to check out Houston's local news archives on the internet.

Carol entered from the bedroom where she'd been dressing for work, "How was your run this morning?" she asked innocently.

Relieved that she didn't want to argue Lane answered "I'm still a little stiff, but I'll be ok. I just want to get my last week of work out of the way so we won't have to argue about it any more."

"Who's arguing?" Carol snapped back a little too quickly.

Lane winced. The day after Lane's return he told Carol about the fictitious discussion with his 'boss', explaining that he put in a two week notice. The notice included an agreement to give estimates on four more roofs.

"No!" Carol demanded, her concern exploding into fury. "No! Not again! Not after what just happened to you. Are you crazy? Are you *trying* to get yourself killed?"

The words cut quick and clean . . . and deep. As if she knew exactly what Lane had really been doing, what he still had to do! At first he was stunned speechless, his words caught in his throat and Carol's words hammered him inward toward the waiting chaos . . . .

Something clicked within his psyche then his thoughts fell into order and the confusion cleared. Lane's clenched fist slammed hard onto the table where the two held their discussion, cutting Carol off in the middle of whatever she'd been saying.

"Enough!" Lane shouted jumping to his feet, knocking the chair over behind him. "Don't you raise your voice at me, woman!" Lane growled through clenched teeth, his face contorted by rage, "I've made an agreement and I'll keep to it. I've given my notice just like any other job would expect. Is that understood?"

Carol simply nodded, not looking up from the table, knowing that anything she said or did would be a useless, wasted effort. At least, she thought to herself, it would be his last job. Lane snapped again almost instantly. What was he doing? He thought.

Sagging his shoulders he sighed, "You're right, I'm sorry." he said softly.

He took Carol in his arms, but the embrace was strained at best. "It's my last time to go baby. Please try to understand that I'm trying to be a better person that I was in the past, for us. Part of being that person is to do what I've given my word to do instead of just walking away a quitter."

Carol looked up into Lane's eyes then nodded, "ok, baby. I love you, so you better not hurt yourself again."

The two shared a short kiss and the tension between the couple subsided a bit.

* * *

A few days later, Lane was still sore from the beating he endured at the hands of the bikers. He'd been searching the newspapers and news stations archives on the internet to see if LeGross had been found yet, when the door bell rang. Lane signed offline and, not considering who could be at his door, opened the portal swinging the door wide. A myriad of emotions ranging from confusion to worry to rage slammed into Lane's chest as he stared blank faced into the eyes of Detective Von Eric.

"Morning, Mr. Bryant. May I come in?" The detective asked with a smile.

Lane barely heard the question as the carousel of voices in his head began spinning out of control, creating a vortex from which a raging chaos was released. Von Eric looked at Lane curiously not knowing of the inner turmoil ripping through his psyche.

"Bryant?" Von Eric asked again worriedly, not understanding how close he was standing to his own demise.

Quietly, with an unnerving calm, Lane answered, "You're a little out of your jurisdiction, detective."

Taken aback some what, Von Eric stated, "Your wife wouldn't talk to me so I had to drive . . ."

"My wife wouldn't talk to you because you didn't have a warrant, Von Eric. If you don't have a warrant now, this could be seen as harassment. Do you have a warrant, detective?"

Lane was being intentionally spiteful and rude, but he knew that if a warrant had been issued then Harris County would have just called the local police like they've done before.

"Do your superiors know where you are, Von Eric?" Lane asked harshly.

Von Eric's shoulders slumped a bit, then Lane not willing to let another word escape Von Eric's lips, stated flatly "I suggest, if you ever come to my door again that you learn how to read!"

This caused Von Eric to look at Lane confused. Lane then pointed to the door mat just outside the apartment door which the detective stood on. Von Eric took a step back to reveal a light beige mat with a simple dark border. The words on the mat were in bold black letters,

**'COME BACK
WITH A
WARRANT!'**

Von Eric looked back to Lane not hiding the anger in his face. Lane slammed the door hard then engaged the dead bolt with a loud 'click'.

Not a little agitated, Von Eric made the two hour trip back to Houston with no more answers than he had that morning.

* * *

The time crept by slowly as Lane allowed himself to heal. During those days, Lane learned District Attorney Keith LeGross had been found by an investor who'd been surveying the warehouse property for purchase. There had been hints of a federal investigation, but there had been no confirmation. Lane decided no matter how this trip turned out, it would be his last trip to Houston. As Bryant's truck sped toward his destination so did his thoughts. Heading westbound on I-10 Bryant remembered his promise to Marcus Martinez. The attorney, Judge Rights and possibly Von Eric were the only three left to sentence.

Von Eric; that was a tough one! If Von Eric wasn't involved with sending Lane to prison, if he was in fact opposed to it, then Lane would be no better than the ones he was sentencing. Still, Von Eric was a cop! And Lane had never before met a *good* cop. Every cop had his hand in some dirt, somewhere. Von Eric was no different! Yet everyone Lane asked about the detective has attested to his honor. Lane finally decided that he couldn't pursue Von Eric, but he may have become a liability. If Von Eric ever showed himself again, Lane would have to kill him regardless of the cop's involvement with Lane's prosecution.

Another difficult task would be Judge 'Big Time' Bill Rights. Lane truly dreaded sentencing the judge. The possibility of a federal investigation into the death of the late Keith LeGross would become a certainty with the death of Judge Rights. There could be no contact with Rights. No explanation about why he would die *and* he would be denied the right to face his accuser.

Lane couldn't risk a federal investigation. He feared that the feds were way out of his league. They would search all nooks and crannies searching for a lead and who knows what type of technology and training those guys have. Lane considered his conversation with Osbourne. Was the late detective so naïve to believe that Lane would do any favors for him? Sure it would be good to expose the judge's criminal activities, but that's beside the point of *Lanes* mission. The idea that Osbourne would even trust Lane was ludicrous and why would the former detective even give a damn whether or not those records came into the open?! After all it wouldn't benefit him, he's dead . . .

Lane veered recklessly to the shoulder of the highway, nearly forcing another vehicle off the road and cutting off several others. Once on the shoulder, Lane slammed on the brakes, jammed the gears into park and killed the engine. His mind was racing in panic and his breath evaded his pursuit. Light headed Lane exited the truck and made his way to the tailgate. After a while, Lane was able to calm down and come to terms with the possibility he now faced. He kept repeating the scene of Osbourne's death over and over in his mind; could the son of a bitch have switched pills. Sure he *could* have, but *did* he? Of course he did, what idiot would willingly swallow cyanide!! And what idiot would believe he could *force* someone take it!

Lane sat on the tailgate with his head hung low. *Damn* he thought; that bastard is alive and there's no way to find him. Lane leaned back into the bed staring at the sky's crystal blue infinity. He knew at that moment that he was a dead man, and unless some marvelous twist of fate killed Osbourne then the late detective would be coming for him. The only question was when, and how. Lane made himself focus on the task at hand; he couldn't let himself be distracted by thoughts of Osbourne. Besides, Osbourne needed Lane to retrieve those records isn't that right. Lane kills Rights and gets the records; Osbourne then kills Lane and takes over Rights business. Great! Lane had no intentions of getting those records from Rights, now he sure as hell ain't gonna mess with them. Osbourne won't interfere with Lane until the judge is dead.

Finally Lane stood and closed the tailgate. "So Martinez," Lane mumbled to himself, "I suppose it's *your* turn."

Lane checked into a hotel in north Houston near the Bush International Airport, then immediately drove to a pay phone in south Houston. The only phone he could use to contact Trigga, Lane's supplier. After the call he continued to a small warehouse district in a deteriorating part of the city. Lane waited patiently, sitting on the tailgate in an abandoned building. An hour ticked by before a young kid of about thirteen years entered at the far end. His spotless white clothes seemed to glow in contrast to the kid's dark skin.

"You da man?" The kid asked sneering at Lane, who already didn't like the kid.

Probably some local hood, Lane thought cynically, who's got more bullets than brains; and definitely more bullets that Lane who was unarmed at the moment.

"I'm no cop kid! Where's your boss?"

After a moment of staring at one another across the empty warehouse, the kid obviously sizing up the white man unsure whether to believe him, he raised the garage door just enough to allow a S.U.V. to enter unscathed. The heavily tinted, black Escalade stopped nearly twenty yards from where Lane sat patiently. A large mountain of a man exited the front passenger door standing at an easy six and a half feet. The man's eyes, dark as his skin and sharp as a hawk, roamed through the empty building in search of any prey that may be hiding in the darkness, before focusing intently on Lane. The predator's large frame gracefully moved around the open door toward Lane, revealing the muscled mass of a professional defensive lineman.

Towering over Lane the large man made a motion indicating that Lane should allow himself to be searched. Lane complied, agitated but silent, and once the lineman was satisfied with his search he nodded toward the young hood at the garage door. The kid closed that door then took his post at the smaller door from which he entered, while the larger man took up post at the passenger front tire of the S.U.V. The driver then exited the vehicle, taking his post at the rear tire on that side of the S.U.V. In unison, both rear doors opened and Lane heard the sound of shoes fall, but saw no one. Two very short men became visible on each side of the Escalade and seemed to waddle more than walk toward Lane, who was grinning broadly at the duo.

"What's so funny, D?" Trigga asked, feigning anger.

"Oh, nothing. Nothing at all." Lane said reaching down to shake the dwarf's hand.

"This is my brotha, Dino." Trigga stated flatly, introducing his identical twin.

The two shook hands. Lane's order was reletatively small so he had to ask, "Why all the security? What's on your mind?"

The twins glanced at each other then Trigga said flatly, "Let's take care of business first. Then we'll talk about . . . other issues."

Lane and Trigga went way back, so he wasn't concerned with a double cross. Whatever the twins wanted to discuss was serious and Lane instinctively understood that it had to do with the reason he was in Houston.

"Alright, business first," Lane said after a short moment. "You got my goods?"

Without missing a beat Dino shot back, "Got my money?"

Anger flashed across Lane's features followed by a quick smile. From his rear pocket Land produced and envelope and, with a quick look to Trigga, tossed it to Dino. Without counting the bills, or even looking to see if there was cash inside, Dino looked to the S.U.V. and held it up. The lineman at the front tire returned to the cab and retrieved a mid size duffle bag, delivered the bag to the dwarf then returned to his post.

Dino set the bag on the tailgate and began removing its contents. "Two Beretta nine millimeters, suppressed. Six extra extended clips, three boxes of ammo, two stealth holsters adapted for suppressed weapons and one under garment bullet proof vest."

Lane examined the supplies for a moment before he realized the twins were staring at him. "What is it?"

Dino was the first to speak. "A little something extra we pitched in for you. Just for principal."

Lane glared at the twins for a long moment. Nothing is free, *ever*.

"What's the little something extra, and what's the principal you're following." Lane didn't try to hide his irritance.

Dino continued, "One H & K socom forty-five caliber subsonic pistol with integrated laser sight and whisper lock special."

Lane couldn't hide his surprise at the hardware. A whistle escaped without his knowledge.

"The subsonic means that it's already suppressed, but with the use of the whisper lock, it will be *completely* silent. That feature is only good for one round before you have to reset it. Here's two additional extended clips, two boxes of ammo and this." Dino finished by handing Lane a cell phone.

Confused Lane asked the obvious, "You're giving me a cell phone?"

Trigga said "That's no cell phone."

Lane looked at the phone, turning it over in his had. Then he looked at Trigga for an explanation, then to Dino who smiled and answered, "It's a trigga."

Dino removed the final item, a small clear package. Wrapped tightly within the plastic was an identical cell phone with wires protruding from its insides and plugged into a wad of grey colored putty.

"Three quarter block of C-4 explosive, rigged to explode when its phone rings." Dino handed the package to Lane. Astonished, having never before been in possession of anything like this, Lane remained speechless.

The dwarf continued, "On the back side are industrial strength adhesive strips. You can stick that puppy to any damn thing. Both phone batteries are fully charged and *this* phone," Dino indicated the packaged phone, "is programmed to deny any call from any phone except *that* one." Again Dino indicated the first phone he handed to Lane.

"Just turn the phone on, stick the package to wherever you want then get the hell away. To detonate the package, hold down the number one for speed dial. Then boom!"

Lane inspected the H & K and the C-4 enthusiastically for several minutes. Then his smile faded into a blank expression. Looking at Trigga Lane simply asked, "Why?"

Trigga stepped up to Lane, motioning him to lean in so he would hear the whisper.

"There was a certain D.A. who came to an obviously painful and very humiliating end . . ."

Interrupting the little man, Lane stood and in a hushed voice instructed, "Be careful with what you *think* you know little man!"

Dino immediately reached to the small of his back where, Lane guessed, he had a gun tucked. Trigga held out a hand toward his brother, shaking his head.

He looked to Lane scornfully. "Don't believe for one second that you can come to *my* city, pull a hit like that and expect me not to find out who it was!"

Of course, Lane thought to himself, how could I think that I'd possibly get away with killing a district attorney? Arrogance? Stupidity is more likely the reason. Now he was going after a *judge* for Christ sake! Apparently his stupidity knows no bounds! Lane noticed the twins were staring at him solemnly.

"What's happened?" He asked cynically.

Trigga glanced at this brother who held his stare at Lane, "TAC is looking for you." Dino stated bluntly.

"Who the fuck is Tac?" Lane said angrily, "And where do *I* find *him?*"

"Not him" Dino said, "Them!" he paused to let that sink in for a moment.

"The Texas Aryan Coalition. They want the one who killed two of their bros and they want him dead. They're pissed and they're heavily armed. They ain't friendly and they don't play fair."

"Shit!" Lane's thought became audible.

"Yeah!" The twins echoed in unison.

Trigga continue, "Keep the four-five close; I'm on that speed dial, number three. If there's a way for me to help when the shit hits the fan, I will. If they find out it's you, you're gonna need all the help you can get."

After a long silence, Trigga quietly nodded, slapped his twin on the shoulder and then left Lane sitting alone on the tailgate considering his options. *Shit!*

Osbourne. TAC. "Who the fuck's next?" Lane wondered aloud.

Slamming the tailgate shut, Lane was determined to finish what he set out to do and let the pieces fall where they may.

* * *

The next morning, after the shock from the recent news he acquired had worn off, Lane purchased a small two door foreign car using one of his aliases. He then went to the outskirts of the Montrose area to a market district commonly used by the area's drag queens and male prostitutes. A small trick he'd learned in his past, if you want to confuse your pursuer don't just change your appearance, change your gender. The trick proved invaluable in his youth, now it could possibly save his life.

Dressed in a thigh-high skirt, shorts underneath, an inexpensive blouse and women's Nikes, Lane sat in his new Audi on the third floor of a multi-leveled parking garage that serviced the building where his former court appointed attorney held his office. Lane's attire was complete with stockings to hide his hairy legs, heavy make-up applied by a beautician to hide any evidence of his recently shaved facial hair, one long haired wig, painted finger nails, a small amount of jewelry including a choker necklace intended to disguise Lane's protruding Adam's apple and a modest C-cup size pair of fake breasts, which he wore over the bullet proof vest. The vest and C-cups caused the blouse he wore to fit much tighter. This seemed to enhance the effect of the fake breasts, giving him a more 'womanly' appearance.

As Lane waited for Martinez to leave his office for the day, concerns about the twins figuring him out, the possibility of the TAC set discovering his identity, the visit from Von Eric and the possibility of Osbourne's survival began to invade his thoughts. Concern transformed into doubt causing him to again second guess his confidence.

"Don't think about it, just *do* it!"

Lane snapped from his contemplation as violently as if someone had slapped him.

"Hesitation will kill you!"

Lane frantically looked around the interior of the car before the realization that it was his own voice who spoke to him. His anxiety peaked; Lane looked into the mirror mounted on the windshield.

His voice trembled as he spoke to the angered reflection snarling back at him, "Leave me alone! I'm taking care of this and I don't need your help."

In a condescending tone the angry voice replied, "You'll always need me, even now you're thinking about backing out of this. That, I will *not* allow!"

The following smile seemed to spawn from pure evil rather than arrogance, but it quickly vanished, being replaced by a timid expression of uncertainty. Lane's next words were caught short before a sound could find its purchase, his mouth slowly closed to match the grim expression which spread throughout his features. Marcus Martinez had appeared from the far end of the garage, near the office building.

Lane started his car, exited the garage onto a one way street then pulled to the curb before the first corner, waiting for Martinez to follow. A moment later the attorneys expensive luxury sedan passed by.

"Wait!" Lane's harsh voice demanded.

He glanced at his mirrored image which continued its instruction. "Give him a few blocks lead, than follow carefully. Don't get any closer than a few car lengths. He can't get away!"

Lane did exactly that but soon the two vehicles entered the 610 Loop. Lane realized that Martinez wasn't headed to his home; he headed toward down town instead.

An exotic café was tucked between a five story building that housed expensive condos and a row of various gift and specialty shops. The five story condo building stood prominently at the intersection of two wide, lightly traveled streets. Lane eased to a stop at the crossroads where his prey had turned, looking in the same direction. It at first appeared that Martinez would veer his car right through the front glass of the café, but the vehicle seemed to melt into the ground just before impact.

Lane quickly navigated the corner to discover a ramp that descended underneath the café. He followed the attorney's lead and found himself in an underground parking garage. Lane guessed that it serviced the five story building above. He also guessed that if he didn't take care of Martinez now he'd be waiting for a long time, maybe all night.

"To hell with this shit!" Lane growled to himself as he exited his car.

Across the garage, Lane watched as Martinez entered an elevator and he began running to catch up before the doors shut. Lane couldn't cross the distance fast enough and the elevator shut just as he arrived.

"Damn!" he whispered, kicking the double doors. Lane turned to leave when he heard the doors opening. He smiled to himself thinking if Martinez only knew what he just did to himself.

"You almost missed it." Martinez said smiling.

Lane, his back to the elevator, withdrew one of his suppressed Berettas. "Yeah, thanks Marcus."

Martinez' smiling face faded into an expressed confusion when he heard his first name spoken in a man's voice. Then that expression transformed into terror and unbelief when Lane, moving too quick for Martinez, spun around and landed the butt of the nine millimeter across his forehead. The well placed blow knocked Martinez to the floor in a daze. Wasting no time, Lane kicked Martinez hard in the ribs forcing the breath from his lungs.

Then placing the barrel of the gun under Martinez' chin, Lane spoke calmly, "Do you know who I am Marcus? Do you remember?"

Martinez tried to focus his swimming vision toward the image in front of him.

"Look at *me* you piece of shit!" Lane demanded.

Obviously dazed, Martinez only shook his head.

"Focus Marcus!" Lane instructed. "Judge Rights' court room nearly six years ago." Lane paused. "Bryant! My name is Lane Bryant!"

Martinez' eyes focused and locked with Lane's; recognition evident in his face.

"That's right you worthless fuck! I told you I'd get you! Didn't I, you crooked bastard!"

Lane followed his words with another vicious kick to Martinez' stomach then stepped on the attorney's hand, pointed his weapon at the man's face and demanded, "Which floor punk?"

When Martinez didn't immediately answer Lane stomped his hand, "I said which floor!"

Growls of pain issued from Lane's prey, but he managed to show four digits with his other hand. Lane pressed the button to begin the ascent and pulled Martinez to his feet by his hair.

"You let anyone in this box, I'll kill you both! You can survive this," Lane lied, "if you play by my rules, understood?"

Martinez nodded silently and the two rode up to the fourth floor.

When the elevator opened Lane whispered into the attorney's ear, "Any tricks and your dead. Let's get to where you were headed so we can talk."

Lane stayed a few feet behind Martinez allowing the attorney to lead him down the short hall and around a corner to the third door.

When Martinez stopped he mumbled, "This is it."

"Good, ring the bell and get us out of this hall!" Lane instructed calmly and stepped out of the view of the door's peephole.

Lane waited for what seemed like and eternity after the door bell sounded. Finally, he heard the lock disengage and quickly grabbed Martinez by the collar of his suit shoving him into the room as the door opened.

"Marty!" A woman's voice rebounded from within, surprised. "What's wrong with . . ."

The beautiful redhead gasped as she was forced deeper into her condo. Inside, gun in full view, Lane locked the dead bolt using a handkerchief he pulled from a pocket in the skirt he wore, never moving his eyes from his captives. Lane motioned with the gun for the two to leave the short hallway into the living area. The woman began to yell until he fired a round into the wall beside her.

"That's the only warning you get bitch. Now move!" Lane whispered.

Once out of the dim lit foyer, Lane noticed how alluring the woman was. Apparently the coupe only had one thing in mind when Martinez arrived for the woman only wore a black nightie of see through fabric, which fell high on her thighs. Her large pink nipples strained at the thin material which was tightened even more by her ample breasts. Lane couldn't help but notice that the only hair on the woman's body was the lustrous red hair on her head.

"Wow!" Lane mumbled unconsciously bringing a blush to the clear milky skin of the woman's cheeks.

She immediately covered her breasts as best she could with one arm and hairless public region with her other hand.

"Sit down!" Lane demanded, "Right there!" he indicated the floor in the middle of the room.

From the back of a nearby love seat, Lane tossed the woman a small blanket to cover herself with. Her lack of dress, Lane knew, would be a distraction that he couldn't afford at the time.

Staring at Martinez Lane stated, "You sold me out counselor, now you're gonna pay."

Lane then fired two suppressed rounds into Martinez' abdomen which caused him to double over, fall to his side and wrap his arms around his midsection in an attempt to ease the pain. The woman next to him flinched at the quiet shots, but then became possessed with a calmness that seemed to Lane to be out of place.

Before Lane could pin point what exactly was amiss with the woman, Martinez spoke up. "You . . . you shot me . . . you said . . . you wouldn't."

Lane's focus returned to the injured attorney, "That's right Marcus! And now I'm gonna watch you bleed to death unless you tell me exactly what I want to know, understand."

Completely focused on his prey Lane didn't notice the shift in the woman's position. He began questioning Martinez harshly.

"Tell me who Bill Rights and Keith LeGross work for!" Lane demanded.

Horror filled the attorney's features. "They'd kill me if I told you." Martinez whined through his pain.

Disgusted, Lane eyed the man for a long moment. "Look at yourself, Martinez. You're already dead. The only way to save yourself is to tell me what I want to know."

Martinez pressed his wound in an attempt to stop the flow of blood. Pitifully he whined, "They call themselves the Texas Aryan Coalition . . . Urrgh!"

Lane kicked Martinez in the groin. "I know that, you fuck! *Who* are they? Who's in charge? Give me his name!" He demanded.

Lane stepped in to kick the attorney again, but as he stepped the woman exploded with a powerful forward kick into Lane's groins. When Lane bent forward from the blow he was met with a heel to his chin which sent him sprawling backward. Before he was on the floor his attacker was on her feet. When he hit the floor, he felt his weapon being kicked from his grasp. Lane instinctively rolled away from the blow, leaving his gun wherever it landed. He quickly came off the floor into a crouched position on one foot, but the beautiful red head was too fast for him.

Throwing the small blanket over Lane as he rose to his feet, the woman laced her fingers behind his head. Holding Lane in a bent position with the blanket over him, she kneed him in the face once . . . twice. Before she could place another blow, Lane reached out from under his veil and grabbed the ankle on the leg that she stood on and jerked it out from under her. The woman fell to the floor hard pulling the blanket with her.

Able to see now, Lane spotted Martinez dragging himself toward the loose pistol lying on the carpet. Lane took the two steps to close in on Martinez, kicking him hard in the jaw. An audible 'pop' issued throughout the room indicating the jaw had broken.

Lane reached down to pick up the weapon, but it was kicked away before he could grab it. Instinctively, he pulled the second pistol he brought, but as he brought it around the woman landed a well placed kick to his temple. Numbed by the blow, Lane could only feel his other weapon being knocked from his grip.

His vision cleared just in time for him to fend off a flurry of blows brought on by the beautiful red head. The training the woman had apparently gone through surprised Lane. Her calculated attacks set Lane on his heels, though he could feel his attacker losing power and speed.

One of her attacks broke through his defenses again hitting him in his temple. In a blind rage, Lane reached up and grabbed a handful of flowing red hair, violently jerking his attacker's head back as far and hard as he could. The woman gasped painfully as her head snapped back from the force of Lane's rage. Seeing the woman defenseless, Lane slammed his white knuckled fist into her throat with all his might, crushing her larynx. The woman couldn't even grasp for breath, her throat being completely sealed.

Lane's vision went from blurred to black as the woman's eyes bulged and she grasped at her neck. Out of control, Lane unconsciously jerked his attacker around by her hair leading her toward the closed patio door that led onto the balcony. With her hair in one hand, Lane reached between the woman's legs forcing her headlong through the glass door, onto the balcony and over the railing . . .

Lane heard a horn sound in the distance drawing him from a land of darkness. The world around him seemed to slowly circle into reality as he looked down at the scene below. People on the street were pointing at him on his fourth story perch. Others were standing over the crumpled body of a nearly nude woman. Bright red tracks of blood trailed a city bus, which evidently had run over the poor girl after her four story plunge.

Staring at that scene everything came rushing back to Lane in an instant. Spinning away from the edge of the balcony, Lane quickly and carefully reentered the condo. Diving into a roll behind the love seat, Lane heard Martinez trying to speak through his ruined jaw. Lane peeked around the seat to discover Martinez trying to speak into the phone. Taking note that he attorney didn't hold one of Lane's missing weapons; he ran to the phone and jerked the wire from the wall. Martinez, too weak to fight, just looked at Lane pleadingly. Lane found his weapons, holstering one then returned to Martinez.

"Who'd you call?" Lane demanded.

Martinez gurgled a wet, weak laugh then spoke as best he could with his broken jaw, "Well," he laughed a little more, "You wanted to meet them."

"Shit!" Lane said urgently helping Martinez to his feet and guiding him toward the exit. "Open it, you son of a bitch!" Lane growled pressing the attorney's face against the door.

Lane pushed Martinez into the hall way ahead of himself. Before the ring of gunfire registered to Lane, Martinez was being hit with round after round. The hail of lead sent Martinez into an involuntary dance, the impact of the rounds animating his performance. Lane never looked up and, letting go of Martinez, he sprinted down the hall using the dancing corpse as his cover. By the time Martinez' body fell to the floor, Lane was in the stairwell descending the stairs two at a time.

Covering the sound of his descent was the fire alarm that had been triggered when Lane pushed through the exit into the fire escape. He descended past the third floor door onto the landing between the third and second floors. Trying to catch his breath, Lane crouched into the corner and tried to force his eyes adjust to the flashing strobe of the fire alarm. After a quick rest he withdrew his second pistol then proceeded down the exit more cautiously. The noise of a door clicking shut sounded out, breaking the rhythm of the alarm. Not able to hear any foot falls, Lane guessed that he wouldn't be heard either. Hurrying past the landing between the second and first floors toward the garage, Lane caught sight of a flash of light independent of the flashing strobe. The light flashed just before a small explosion erupted from the concrete wall next to his head.

Without thinking, moving purely on instinct, Lane pitched himself into a forward roll down the steps as he fired one simultaneous round from each of his pistols. Landing at the first floor fire exit, Lane pressed his back to the door looking around wildly for his pursuer. Panic rose within Lane when he couldn't locate the source of the bullet that nearly took his head off. As his panic started to mount, Lane spotted a gun laying on the first step below the landing where he crouched. Lane's eyes followed the steps down to the next landing.

"Oh, fuck!" He whispered in awe.

On the steps near the next landing laid an officer of the Houston Police department.

"Oh, fuck!" Lane whispered again as the realization of who he just killed registered in his mind.

Lane descended the steps slowly. The officer laid on the step with his head bent at an unnatural angle on the landing itself. It seemed to Lane that the rounds he fired, knocked the cop back down the steps, breaking his neck in the fall.

Osbourne, TAC and now the cops would want him dead. "Shit!" Lane said aloud.

He knew that he'd never be arrested. If he was caught, he was *dead*. Caution to the wind, Lane fled down the remaining steps, slamming through the door into the underground parking garage below. Desperate to get away from the area, Lane sprinted across the garage to his car. As the sound of the slammed door echoed down the corridor, the sound of shattering glass rebounded from Lane's left. Immediately, Lane dove between a pair of cars to his right, landing in a roll and coming up into a crouch. Ending the improvised maneuver, Lane found himself staring down the barrel of gun.

Not willing to die without a fight, Lane whispered a silent prayer for his family then, to keep from lifting his arms, he slowly bent his writs upward and fired both weapons. A round from one of the suppressed pistols cut into the other man's stomach and exited through his shoulder, rending that arm useless. The other round caught the man under his chin, exiting through the back of his skull. The man fell backwards, hard.

Lane stared at the dead man for a long moment not moving, not even breathing. His mind tried to grasp the fact that he wasn't dead, but the fact continued to evade him. Lane *was* dead and he knew it! Yet, he still breathed.

"Hey Tweak?! You get him?" A hushed call came from somewhere down the corridor toward the elevators.

Lane remained motionless, breathing quietly and listening intently. Precious seconds ticked away with the heartbeats of a jackrabbit and Lane felt the pressure of lost time. He had to get out of there, and soon. The wail of sirens rose in the distance as though some supernatural intelligence, possessed with a twisted sense of humor, had known Lane's despairing thoughts and tormented him with the fears. Whatever game Lane was caught in, one thing was certain his time was up and he had to get out of there, *now*!

Fortunately for Lane, the man seeking for Tweak felt the panic also.

"Shit!" came a muffled remark from much closer than before and was followed by receding foot falls.

Lane didn't waster another second; sprinting the remaining distance to his car, he hurried from the garage and around the corner.

* * *

Lane slowed to a stop at the curb a couple of blocks away from the scene as a fire truck, followed by an ambulance and a couple of H.P.D. squad cars, passed with their sirens blaring. Once the vehicles went by Lane's Audi, he began to ease away from the curb watching the rearview closely. One of the squad cars slammed on its breaks and slid sideways into a u-turn followed shortly by the other.

"Fuck!" Lane cursed aloud stomping down on the accelerator.

The sports sedan leaped into action, spinning its tires for just a moment as Lane peeled away. He sped down the lightly populated street, adjusting the head set he purchased for Trigga's cell phone. The two squad cars gained on Lane fast and were nearly on top of him, one positioning itself for a 'pit maneuver'. Lane wasn't about to let that happen. At speeds of sixty to seventy miles, Lane suddenly and recklessly navigated a right turn onto a crossroad. The Audi handled tightly and took the maneuver easily, sliding only slightly until Lane released the throttle and allowed the vehicle's traction to find its purchase again. Then he jammed the accelerator to the floor once more.

The pursuing police units were unprepared tor Lane's tactic and sped straight through the intersection. One, however, came to a screeching halt. Throwing the transmission into reverse, the police unit backed its way to the cross street. White smoke and the smell of burning rubber filled the air as the car's front end slid around to point in the direction of the Audi. Even as that squad car leaped forward in pursuit, its counterpart rounded the corner a few blocks away heading the same direction.

Lane began zigzagging through the city, taking another right for a couple of blocks before cutting back to the left on another street.

"Trigga, the shit just hit the fan!" Lane yelled into the headset.

Listening intently to Trigga's instructions, answering questions when asked, Lane guided the Audi along at dangerous speeds, zigzagging his way toward the nearest interstate. He approached the busy highway thinking that he had evaded his pursuers. But as he passed the last cross road before reaching the interstates feeder, a squad car slid around the corner almost ramming the Audi in its side. Lane countered at the last second, veering into the oncoming lane and putting the curbed median between himself and his pursuer. The squad car sped past Lane into the intersection at the interstate's overpass and slid to a stop, blocking Lane's path.

Lane, however, anticipated the unit's tactic; cutting through a gas station's lot and onto the feeder he headed against traffic. The police unit again leaped forward in pursuit, followed shortly by its lost counter part.

* * *

"Get the boys over to the Beltway and forty-five, *now*!" Trigga yelled as he descended the stairs. "Bring the rockets!"

Dino jumped from the sofa where him and one of his crew were gambling on a football game they'd been playing on the Play Station 3. He hurried from the room barking orders into his Nextel radio.

"Black," Trigga continued his instructions to Dino's football opponent, "get the trucks, we've got work to do!"

Black jumped the sofa he'd been sitting in and ran out the front door. Trigga mumbled more instructions into his phone as he hurried out the door behind Black.

* * *

Lane made his way onto Interstate 10 after crossing under its overpass to gain access in the proper direction. At the overpass' intersection, Lane nearly ran down a bum who was crossing the street on crutches and carrying a cardboard sign. The bum had dropped the crutches and dove to the concrete walk, knocking free a wad of bills in varying denominations. The bum chased the loose bills which were blown by gusts of wind caused by the pursuing police cruisers.

Lane pushed the sports sedan as hard as he could onto the northbound Interstate 45. Answering the phone on the first ring Lane spoke with an unworldly calm voice, "I'm on my way! No sign of any choppers yet."

As soon as the words left his lips, Lane saw the mechanical bird rising in the distance. Again, that supernatural intelligence seemed to be playing his twisted games.

"Correction Trigga, I'm hot!" he finished wildly.

The chase continued northbound on Interstate 45 for several minutes. The flowing traffic yielded to the chase as more police units joined the pursuit. As Lane closed in on Beltway 8 North Loop near Greenspoint Mall, he noticed that many of the highway's exits had been closed off.

Good! That's just what he expected.

* * *

In Greenspoint, North Houston, at the intersection of Interstate Highway 45 and Beltway 8, there are several ramps over passing one another at varying heights, angles and directions. This 'spaghetti bowl' made it virtually impossible to get a visual of a vehicle on the ground level from a helicopter. That is exactly the reason why Trigga chose the area. His crew blocked off several of the exits from the highway, leaving the lower feeder roads and turn-arounds deserted. Lane understood the method and was relieved to see it set up so quickly.

Lane exited the interstate, smashing through a roadblock set up by Trigga's crew, with five squad cars and a helicopter in pursuit. Slowing as he came to the intersection on the ground level, well out of the view of the pursuing helicopter, Lane made a quick left turn and came to a screeching halt. As he braked, Lane jerked the steering wheel to the right causing the Audi to slide sideways to block as much of the road as possible.

As the first squad car rounded the corner in pursuit, a rocket whistled across the wide intersection trailing a thin line of white smoke. Exploding into its target, the rocket caused the squad car to jump into the air. The remaining four police cruisers slid to a halt as the fifth vehicle bounced from the ground in a ball of fire.

The carnage rang out in deafening explosions as Lane bailed from the Audi with his gear and ran toward six black Escalade S.U.V.'s that were parked nearby. The nearest one waited with the back door open.

Inside the truck, Lane watched one of Dino's crew toss a grenade into his Audi, destroying the vehicle and any evidence that could be traced back to him. Instantaneously, two more rockets let loose. One streaked into a police cruiser, whose driver fled the vehicle. The force of the explosion pitched the officer headlong onto the road where he stayed, motionless.

The other shot skyward. The helicopter pilot took evasive action, but it was too late. Just as the aircraft tilted into its maneuver, the tail was clipped at the rudder and severed from the bird by the ensuing explosion. Black and white smoke twisted together following the chopper's downward spin. Colliding into nearby Greenspoint Mall, the helicopter exploded, destroying Dillard's department store and igniting a fire within the complex.

"Let's go, let's go, let's go!" Trigga commanded into his Nextel!

The remaining members of the twin's crews jumped into the other vehicles then, in unison, all six identical Escalades fled the area in different directions.

* * *

Once Trigga was satisfied that they had escaped, he turned around in his seat and eyed Lane.

"What the 'fuck' you wearing?" He asked incredulously. Removing the wig, Lane simply said, "Disguise."

The dwarf watched as Lane transformed his image.

"Shit, man! Never thought of that! And those punks have been doin' it for years!"

Lane chuckled as he used the blouse to wipe the make-up from his face. Looking down at his vest he decided that he wasn't ready to part with it.

"I need a large T shirt." He said flatly.

Trigga nodded, "Black, give the man your shirt." Then sizing up both men, he continued, "Your pants and shoes, too."

Sitting next to Lane in the back seat, Black just stared at Trigga with an unpleasant look.

"You heard me nigga! Give 'em up!" The dwarf demanded.

Black grudgingly gave lane the clothes. Trigga handed Lane some folded bills, "When we drop you, go buy some fresh threads that fit a little better. Maybe a cap, too."

Trigga continued, "Listen up! We've gotta get these truck off the streets, so we're dropping you at the west end of the Galleria Mall. Get your shit, get changed and head out the North Side.

"When you get outside, look for a Yellow Cab, number twenty nine seventy eight. The light will be off but one of Dino's guys, Big Baby, will be waiting for you. Probably eating lunch, but he'll be sitting on the trunk. Get in, get back to your truck and get the fuck out of Houston."

"I can't. When I leave I won't becoming back 'ever'."

"That's exactly what I was thinking. Disappear!"

Lane stared at his little friend for a long moment. "I've got one more T." He said flatly.

"*What*!" Trigga responded. "Are you fuckin' stupid? You been smokin' that shit or something'?"

"Or something." Lane stated solemnly. "I've got one more and I won't let him go. Not this one! Not *any* one!"

"Look man. I can't help you any more. You get in a bind; you're on your own!" Trigga pointed at Lane's chest to stress his point. "Get outta town! Do it today!"

"No! I came here to take care of business. That's what I'm gonna do."

"Aw shit, man. You're fuckin' ate up!" Trigga said as he turned to face forward.

The Escalade pulled to the curb on the west side of the Galleria. "You're on your own once Big Baby drops you. Now get out." Trigga said angrily.

Lane exited the SUV and shut the door.

Through the open window, Trigga told him, "Good luck, fool."

Lane nodded and hurried into the mall. At little while later, he was in his hotel room.

* * *

Judge 'Big Time' Bill Rights sat in his courtroom chambers frustrated and worried. The events of yesterday would bring him into the spotlight with the coalition. For better or for worse. The more he learned about what wasn't known the more Rights felt like the spotlight would be for the worse. As time passed by he could sense the walls closing in on him as though he was trapped in the jaws of some monsterous beast. Maybe it was time to leave the country, he thought solemnly to himself.

A knock at his door caused Rights to nearly jump out of his skin. He took a quick moment to regain his composure, then with as much confidence as he could master he spoke.

"Come in."

The door opened to reveal Officer Ron Randall, Judge Rights' bailiff. Rights had known Randall for years and in that time the bailiff had never came to the judge's chamber.

"Can you spare a second, Your Honor?"

"Sure Ron," The judge replied, "I've got a second."

Judge Rights put his pen down and leaned back in his chair.

Randall looked back down the corridor before entering the chamber and quietly closed the door. Again looking at Rights, the bailiff's features turned to ice. The words that Judge Rights heard didn't fit with the face he'd known for so many years.

"The boss says to drive to the New Caney club house after court today." Randall's tone was firm and commanding, sending a jolt of panic through Bill Rights' spine.

His fear compounded with the realization that he has been unknowingly surrounded by TAC. Rights tried to speak; tried to talk his way out of the trip north.

"New . . . New Caney? But . . . But . . . I . . ."

Officer Randall set his jaw and looked squarely into Judge Rights face.

"That's not a request Bill!"

The tone of Randall's voice and his use of the judge's first name infuriated him, but that passed quickly when Rights understanding dawned on him that the choice of words came directly from White himself. Fear gripped the judge once again and in an attempt to hide it he simply nodded, keeping his eyes focused on the desk before him. Randall made a quick nod of understanding and exited the judge's chamber in the same manner in which he'd entered. As soon as the door clicked shut, Rights jumped from his chair, hurrying to lock his chamber door.

New Caney? He thought to himself, a sickening feeling formed in the pit of his stomach. This didn't feel right at all. The only time Rights had been there was when he signed on with the Coalition and accepted his first payment. Even then, he was all but forced into that situation because of the seat he held as a Harris County Judge. Now he wished that he'd never become a judge, much less one involved with the Coalition.

TAC'S clubhouse was more liken to a militia compound. One that would made David Koresh and the Branch Dividian in Waco look like a Girl Scout campsite. The training that took place there would make Bin Laden and his gang look like a bunch of kids playing at the neighborhood park. Being 'summonsed' to the clubhouse was not a 'good' thing, Rights concluded.

* * *

J.T. White, Furor of the Texas Aryan Coalition and Mayor of Houston, sat in his club office surrounded by several of the Coalition's highest ranking officers. Some of the men wore long beards and even longer hair with so many tattoos it was difficult to tell what their true skin tone once was. Others were impeccably dressed and clean shaven with close cropped, military style hair cuts. All were engaged in a soft swarm of conversation revolving around White.

A knock issued from the main door hushing the chatter, and a creaking of hinges followed as the door opened inward.

"Sir, the judge is here." Came a voice through the crowd. "Good." White replied. "You guys know your duty. Get to it!" He commanded and the room emptied, leaving White with his lieutenant general.

Bill Rights was escorted into the small office and left with the two men.

"Sit down Bill." White said firmly.

The judge took the seat across an old wood desk from White. Once Rights settled in, the Coalition's Furor rose from his seat and rounded his desk to pace the span of the small office just behind his guest. Rights' uneasiness grew into discomfort and as the second's ticked away, fear spawned in his heart. Rights expected his life to end then and there and all he could do to hide his terror was stare at White's Lt. Gen.

"Tell me what you've learned so far," White instructed as he slowly paced back and forth.

Rights had prepared himself for this type of questioning. He replayed what his responses would be over and over in his head. He also was prepared to tell the Coalition whatever it wanted to hear to save his neck. All he had to do was buy himself a couple of days to make his get away. Maybe even as early as tomorrow he'd be long gone; hopefully to Spain.

"We've learned several things," Rights began confidently, never removing his eyes from the man in the corner. "Of course, you already know your guy had help escaping the scene and evading the police."

"Guy?" White interrupted." My intel informs me that it's a woman who's causing all the chaos."

Rights nodded quickly, "And several eyewitnesses would confirm that. But the coroner believes that the fist which struck Ms. Lane in her throat was much to large to belong to a woman and *they* say that it would have taken a *very* strong woman to run Ms. Lane *through* a glass door before tossing her far enough off that balcony to land her on the other side of the street.

"What you're telling me, Bill, is that a man dressed himself like a woman to . . . do what?!"

Rights shook his head slowly, "To confuse the police I would guess."

After a short moment, White asked. "Do you have the detectives in our pocket, Bill?"

There it was, the question Rights dreaded the most and the most unavoidable. If the detectives weren't paid off by now then J.T. would expect him to 'replace' them with one of his boys. Rights swallowed the lump that formed in his throat. He could feel the blood rush from his face.

"We've discovered a spot in Detective Von Eric's profile that can be manipulated. We've brought it to his attention with a cash offer. I believe a small application of pressure and a little more cash could seal the deal." Rights lied.

He knew Von Eric would never be bought, or blackmailed. Only replaced and replacement wasn't the judge's specialty. None of that mattered now. By the time J.T. discovered the truth, Rights would find himself tucked safely away in some foreign land surrounded by sexy young girls, far from the Coalition's reach.

Suddenly Rights felt himself being seized by the much stronger Furor. White grabbed the judge from behind by his chin, lifting it high to expose his throat. The cold of a steel blade fell flat against Rights' neck with the razor's edge pointing upward, ready to slice him open. He didn't dare move. He didn't even dare to breathe. White pressed his cheek against the judge's gray hair, positioning his lips to his captive's ear.

"If I don't have a positive I.D. on the fucker who's doing this shit by the first of the week, man or woman, then it'll be *your* head on the chopping block, Bill. Am I making myself clear?" White added a slight more pressure to the knife at Right's throat.

Unable to nod, Rights again forced the lump out of his throat.

"Yeah J.T," he managed weakly, "perfectly clear. I'll find your man!"

"Good." White continued, "I don't care how much it costs, get those detectives in our pocket and bring me what I want!"

White released the judge as suddenly as he'd grabbed him.

"Now get the fuck outta here before I take your balls just for the principal of it." White then looked to his Lt. Gen. "Jim, get that piece of trash outta my sight!"

The man who Rights had been staring at earlier crossed the room, snatched the judge by his collar hoisting him onto his feet then half carried, half shoved him out of the office.

White closed the door behind them and turned to hear the sound of clapping resounding from a nearby, darkened room. As White circled back around his desk toward his seat, a form immerged from within.

"That was very good J.T," the figure spoke as it entered into the light. "I haven't been that entertained in quite some time."

"Shut up Osbourne! You're lucky to be drawing breath yourself!"

Osbourne strolled over to the seat Rights had been sitting in moments before. "Osbourne is dead J.T. Dead and rotting."

"Tell that to the first person to see you on the street."

"Don't worry about that, by this time next week I'll be well underway to having a brand new face to go with my new life. Or should I say, 'I'll be well under the knife'."

The former detective smiled broadly at Houston's own Mayor and the two sat facing one another across the battered desk.

"So detective, what do you say about ol' Bill there?" White asked honestly.

"I think he's full of shit J.T.!" Osbourne replied quickly. White blinked in surprise at Osbourne's blunt remark, but quickly hid his shock.

"Mind explaining that." The Furor commanded.

Osbourne leaned back in his seat. "Well, he's not entirely full of shit. That's definitely no broad you're looking for. He is one ballsy convict though!"

"So, you do know who it is," White inquired.

Osbourne waited a moment trying to decide on just how much to tell the man. "Yeah J.T., I know him."

White stared hard at the former detective. "Why don't you just tell me who he is?" White asked politely.

"I can't do that J.T.

White moved so fast that Osbourne could not have countered quickly enough to save himself if the Mayor/Furor wanted him dead. His unpreparedness had him staring down the barrel of a very large revolver. Osbourne vowed to himself never to let that happen again.

Smiling, White said, "I could just kill you for *not* telling me."

But Osbourne responded with a smirk of his own. "This guy is good J.T., you know it, and he's obviously well connected. Your judge will never finger him, nor will anybody else."

After a moment of consideration, White waved his gun to the side.

"Or I could have my boys beat the info out of you." White half threatened, half teased.

Osbourne's glare was all the response needed. White knew the former detective wouldn't break and he desperately wanted what Osbourne knew.

Holstering the revolver White conceded, "Ok Osbourne. You've proven yourself to be very resourceful and even more stubborn. What do you propose?"

Retrieving a piece of paper from his inner coat pocket, Osbourne smiled. He allowed the Furor to read what was written, as he spoke.

"I'll take care of your guy *and* your judge and I'll take possession of his records. In return I want Bill's cut and a modest slice of that market." Osbourne pointed to indicate the paper in White's hand.

Looking up from Osbourne's writings, White asked, "The judge has been keeping records? . . . That son of a bitch." White wasn't surprised.

"That's not all J.T." Osbourne's smiled broadened again. "Your detective, Von Eric, won't be bought."

The former detective paused to let that settle before he continued. "He won't be bought and he can't be blackmailed." "He's clean J.T. As clean as they come, more so in fact. He lives by some type of higher code." Osbourne made quotation marks with his fingers. "Von Eric's a clean cop that won't compromise."

White leaned forward to rest his elbows on the desk then he rested his chin on his whitening knuckles.

"What are you telling me, Osbourne?"

"I'm telling you that your judge flat bold-face lied to you and I'd have to say, from *my* experience, it seems that he is about to pull one of two stunts."

White could barely hear the former detective through the pounding in his ears. Blood flushed his face and veins throbbed visibly at his forehead. Instead of resting his chin on his knuckles he now massaged his temples.

With his eyes closed tight, White forced his voice through clenched teeth. "Which are?"

Osbourne enjoyed the spectacle, but knew better than to push his luck with this man, so he kept his face blank and his tone flat. Then he simply stated the obvious, "He'll roll over on you or he'll hide somewhere and blackmail you."

White slammed his fist down onto the desk. "Fuuuuck!" The words sounded like the growl of a rabid beast.

Grabbing the right edge of the heavy desk with both hands, White furiously flipped it over to his left. His angered scream rose in volume with each word, "Son. Of. A. BIIITCH!" As the desk crashed onto the floor.

Osbourne sat motionless as the door behind him crashed open and armed men poured inside the room.

White pointed at Osbourne and spittle flew from his lips, as he yelled, "You gotta deal Osbourne! Kill that fucking judge; bring me those records and the head of the bastard who's been fuckin' with my people. Tomorrow night! Be *right here* tomorrow night!" White jabbed a finger at the seat where Osbourne sat as he spoke. Then he stormed out of the office pushing through the crowd that had gathered. Blasts from White's revolver sounded throughout the compound, as Osbourne quietly allowed himself to be escorted away. Tomorrow, Osbourne thought to himself, tomorrow he would begin again.

Chapter Eight

HOMICIDE DETECTIVES FITZGERALD and Von Eric spend most of the night and the following morning investigating the scene at the late Jennifer Lane's condominium complex and the war zone in Greenspoint North Houston, questioning residence and other witnesses.

Back at their office in downtown, the team sat quietly as they researched various statements and reports.

"It's gonna take months to sort through this mess!" Fitzgerald mumbled quietly. "Who, or 'what', in the name of God could cause so much . . . *shit*?" He looked to Von Eric, who appeared to be deep in thought.

"Enis?"

The younger detective looked up. "Oh. Sorry, Norm. I was just thinking the same thing."

Exhausted from the hours of work they'd put in without rest, the pair had talked little about what they'd learned thus far. Piles of papers were scattered across each desk. A T.V. and VCR sat on a stand against a wall with a small stack of tapes from the condo's security cameras. The owners of the condo apparently felt that allowing a Houston Police officer a discounted rent in trade for his experience and services in addition to a few video cameras would be enough security to deter any criminal activity on the premises. The officer who accepted the rental offer was now deceased, having broken his neck in a fall down the stairwell.

"I don't like this Enis!" Fitzgerald said wearily. "She killed a lot of good cops yesterday."

"There's more here than dead cops, Norm." Von Eric said slowly. "And I'm getting the feeling that at least one may not have been acting on behalf of the department."

Fitzgerald, who'd been leaning back in his chair with his feet resting on his desk, stomped them to the floor and sat up straight.

"How can you say that, Enis?!" The detective asked more than a little irritated.

Von Eric matched his partner's irritated glare. All the memories of his past experiences with the late Dave Osbourne flooded his thoughts.

With a forced calm Von Eric flatly stated, "There's something wrong about all this."

Von Eric waved his hands across the office, indicating the stacks of reports, tapes and eye witness accounts.

"I'll start with the obvious, ok?" Von Eric waited for acknowledgement from his partner.

Fitzgerald didn't really want to hear it, but he leaned back into his seat again and gave Von Eric the professional courtesy to speak his mind.

Von Eric started. "There are fourteen rounds, which were fired from four different nine millimeters. Two in the D.O.A., Martinez, one in the dead officer's vest and one that hit the D.O.A found in the garage all match. The other round in the officer's vest also matches the other that hit the D.O.A in the garage.

"That leads me to believe that one person, probably our woman suspect, carried two pistols. The round found in the stairwell matches our officer's police issued nine and the other seven, also found in Martinez, were fired from another pistol altogether. The two rounds in Martinez that matched one found in the officer's vest *and* one that hit our D.O.A. from the garage, were not Mortal wounds. They weren't meant to kill him, while the rounds fired into the D.O.A. in the garage *were* meant to kill. But that was at a close range, very close! I'd say that kill was self-defense because of the forty-four the D.O.A. carried and the angle of the wounds. Whoever killed that guy was on their knees. The rounds pulled from the cars down there didn't match a forty five at all. Those were fired from a thirty-two, which indicates *another* gun man. That's a total of five people with guns, including our dead officer!

"At first I might have guessed a love triangle between the Lane woman, Martinez and this other woman. The woman discovers Martinez is cheating, goes into a jealous rage shooting Martinez and tossing Lane off her balcony. But now, you have some other person filling Martinez full of lead and a D.O.A in the garage who turns out to be," Von Eric picked a sheet of paper from his desk, "a confirmed member from the same gang that owns the club where our late D.A. became missing.

"On top of all that, our dead cop is the only cop on the scene . . ."

"Wait right there!" Fitzgerald interrupted rudely, "That officer lived in that complex! *That's* why he was there!"

Von Eric was already nodding in agreement. "I understand that, Norm; but do you believe that it is probable or even possible, this officer would be able to get as level a shot as he did if he had been falling down the stairs at the same time? The one round he fired is very near head high. A perfect kill, Norm! If I had to guess—and I do have to guess—I'd say it's probable that *he* fired first and when our woman returned fire, the impact knocked him back. He lost his footing and the rest is history.

"Is it procedure to shoot first and *then* try to make an arrest?"

Fitzgerald glared at Von Eric for a moment, "Suppose the officer caught sight of the weapons the woman was carrying. What if she was caught off guard and, when she raised those weapons the officer fired first . . . in self defense."

"Good question, Norm. What would you do in that situation? If you're wearing a vest, would you shoot for the head or for the larger target of the body? If the shot had been aimed for a wound even a mortal wound, instead of a head shot . . ." Von Eric let the rest of his statement hang.

Fitzgerald's glare intensified. He didn't like anybody putting down members of the force—especially one of their own. Yet, Von Eric made some very valid and difficult points, but those only fueled his agitation. Recognizing the senior detective's unpleasant look for what it was Von Eric attempted to ease the harsh reality of it all.

"Norm, I want to give our officer the benefit of the doubt and I admit that I could be way off the mark here. But these facts remain . . . facts."

After a long moment, Fitzgerald nodded his consent to Von Eric's theory. Facts are facts no matter how unpleasant they are, and he knew there was some corruption in the department. It seemed that the dead officer did fire first, and a kill shot at that.

Had the officer tried for a body shot, then he'd probably still be alive and the suspect might even be in custody. The detective didn't even want to consider the probability that other cops would still be alive if that one shot wouldn't have been intended to kill.

"Damn!" Fitzgerald said aloud. "What the *fuck* happened in there?"

Von Eric inserted one the tapes into the V.C.R. "Let's see if these can tell us!" he said in a positive tone.

* * *

The detectives watched the tapes in fast forward except for those parts which seemed relevant to their case. After watching them a second time, Detective Fitzgerald decided he needed to get some rest and called it a day. Alone, Von Eric went through the tapes one more time. He paid close attention to one video in particular. In the scene the female suspect was exiting the parking garage. The monitor showed the driver of the Audi from a few short feet away; however the sun visor was lowered in a position to block the driver's face from the camera's eye. Only the area from the driver's chin to her breasts was visible to the camera. The monitor showed the woman's left hand on the wheel, as though she was about to make a right turn.

The telephone rang and Von Eric paused the tape to answer it. "Fitzgerald's desk, this is Detective Von Eric."

"Enis. It's Clinton, I've got a few things for ya. Are you busy?"

"Nothing that I can't put on hold for a minute, what have you got?"

Clinton worked on the autopsies in the crime lab. Von Eric hadn't expected him to call so soon.

"Well, first I have Ms. Lane. Evidently she took a severe blow to her larynx, before taking her fall. I don't think it was a weapon, meaning that it would have to have been a pretty strong woman to do the damage that was done. Also we've found some glass from the patio door in her hair and some lacerations and a severe knot on her scalp."

"Are you telling me she went through the glass Doc?"

"That's exactly what I'm saying. Again, it would take a damn strong woman to drive someone through that glass. They're a lot thicker these days as compared to what they use to be."

Von Eric looked at the image on the screen. "Is that all Clinton?" He asked slowly.

"As far as the Lane woman is concerned, but I'm surprised you didn't recognize Martinez."

"Why would I recognize him?" Enis asked curiously.

"He used to be the District Attorney here, but he sold out and went into private practice."

Surprised, Von Eric asked, "He's an attorney?"

"Yep!"

For the first time, Von Eric noticed an item on the T.V. screen.

"I have to go Clinton" He said softly.

Without waiting for a response Von Eric slowly lowered the phone, never moving his eye from the image on the T.V.

Staring toward the screen but not seeing it, Von Eric was transported back in time. Suddenly, in his mind's eye, he was standing outside the Bryant residence in Port Arthur . . .

. . . "I suggest, if you ever come to my door again, that you learn how to read! . . .

Lane Bryant's voice sounded clearly in the detective's ears. Von Eric watched in slow motion as Lane raised his hand, again pointing at the welcome mat the detective was standing on. A glint of light reflected from the felon's hand, reflected off of . . . his wedding band . . . a *man's* wedding band.

Von Eric's vision swam back into focus. On the T.V. screen, on the woman's left hand, was her wedding ring. A man's wedding ring . . . *Bryant's* ring!

"Son of a bitch!" Von Eric said full of reverence and fear.

* * *

Lane stayed in his motel room all the next day watching the news. Von Eric, however, searched all of Bryant's files verifying his suspicions about his suspect by listing the names involved with his last conviction.

Roberts, Osbourne, LeGross and now Martinez. That left only Von Eric himself and one other, but would Lane Bryant have the nerve to kill a 'judge'? Or would Bryant come after Von Eric first? One thing was certain, Von Eric would be a lot more careful for awhile. The detective considered Bill Rights for a long while. He should pay the judge a visit to at least give him a warning of the danger he could be in. But that might give him away and scare Bryant off. Even if Von Eric called Rights with a warning it would probably cause the judge to do something he wouldn't normally do and Von Eric decided that he needed Judge Rights to carry on with his everyday life. The plan that was forming in Von Eric's mind was risky. It could turn out to be a waste of time or it could get the judge killed. He didn't like the idea of using Rights as bait, but he didn't have any evidence to make an arrest.

Besides, Bryant would be coming after him or the judge. Von Eric knew it, but if Bryant couldn't find him then he'd go for the judge . . .

"And that's where I'll get you, Bryant." Von Eric mumbled to himself, finalizing his decision.

The following day, Von Eric would begin his surveillance of Judge Rights. Beginning at the Harris County Courts Building; sooner or later Bryant will show himself and Von Eric intended to catch him in the act.

* * *

Chapter Nine

"IMPOSSIBLE!" BRYANT HALF whispered, half growled into the empty night. "This is fucking impossible!"

The sound of Bryant's voice, full of anxiety, echoed back to him softly from the nearby garage annex that serviced the Harris County Courts in downtown Houston. The annex was used exclusively for court employees, namely judges.

The annex was dwarfed by the seventeen story county courts building. Standing only five stories, Bryant figured finding Bill Rights reserved parking spot would be very easy. Sure, Lane thought to himself earlier that afternoon, a judge would have his parking space reserved for him . . . wouldn't he?

During court hours, the garage was patrolled by guards, in addition to the security cameras. At the entrance/exit on the ground floor was a guard station where the guardrails were raised and lowered to prevent or allow vehicles in or out of the garage. Lane had counted three security cameras, one of which continued to pan from left to right taking in the two directions which the vehicles would travel once inside the annex.

At the back of the parking garage in the recesses of a dark alleyway used for trash, Lane stood staring at the six foot chain link fence surrounding the area. Normally, Lane would just climb a fence like this, except this one was topped with a row of razor wire placed to discourage such an action. The point was well taken; He had no intention of getting near that wire. However, cutting a hole in the fence big enough for him to get through was proving to be more difficult than he'd originally thought. In all the books he'd read and all the movies he'd seen, the characters who'd cut through fences like this would do so easily.

"Ain't Hollywood a mother-fucker!" Lane cursed to himself tossing the small bolt cutters to the ground.

He rested the palm of his hands on a nearby metal dumpster, leaning forward so that his head nearly touched the bin.

"I should have brought some better tools!" He mumbled to himself. Suddenly, he smashed his head into the dumpster; "Fuck!" he growled then slammed his head again . . . then again.

"Stop your damn bitchin' and cut that fuckin' hole! I've got no more patience for your whining!" Again Lane heard his voice ricochet softly off the annex wall only this time it was edgy, seemingly full of controlled rage.

Lane labored vigorously to get through the linked barrier and was finally rewarded for his hard work with a hole just barely large enough for him to squeeze through. Knowing that there were no security cameras on the outside of this building, Lane casually walked around the exterior searching for an access point only to discover the only way inside the garage from the ground floor was through the main entrance.

Lane inspected the well lit entrance as best he could from his position in the shadows. He easily spotted two of the three cameras, which he'd seen earlier that day noting that the tiny red light was shining brightly on each camera, indicating they were active. After a few minutes of scrutiny, he determined that there was no way to slip by or even disable the cameras without being caught by the cameras eyes.

Cursing under his breath, Lane back tracked around to the opposite side in hopes to find another way in but with no luck. Frustrated, defeated and both mentally and physically drained, he returned to where he breached the fence. Having a seat on the ground, leaning his back against the exterior wall of the garage, Lane began to wonder what the hell he was doing here at two a.m. and how he could possibly expect to get away with all he'd done. The people of today's society would not view his actions as a form of justice but as the raging of a mad man. If he was lucky he'd get life in a mental institution. What kind of *sane* man would dress like a woman in order to commit murder?

But Lane never believed in good luck, the only luck that came his way was beyond bad, cursed even. The system would probably even put a hold on what society calls humane executions and revert back to medieval times just so they could draw and quarter him, or burn him alive, or something of a more horrendous nature.

Sitting against the wall with knees drawn up to his chest and his head resting on his knees, Lane felt his eyes moistening and forming tears. He immediately caught himself blinking back the tears with the mind set to give up this whole crazy idea, even his vengeful alter-ego was at a loss and therefore quieted. Sighing, he lifted his head to gaze at the starless sky . . .

There! A movement in the corner of his eye. What *was* it? . . . Where'd it go?

There it was again!

A few feet high on the wall a drop of water fell to the ground. One single drop and then another.

Lane stood facing the building, to get a better look. About five feet out of Lane's reach was a small round tube extending out from the garage. It must be a drain for some mechanical unit inside. Lane thought if he can find something to stand on, he could get hold of that drain and use it to get a handhold on the second story ledge. He looked around frantically then ran around to one side of the building and, not finding anything he could stand on, ran back around the other side. There, not far from the entrance, mounted to the wall was an electrical box. The mounted box was centered in a niche along the wall, which was recessed approximately two feet into the building and approximately four feet wide.

Grabbing the top of the box, Lane placed a foot against the two foot wall of the niche and hefted himself up. After a few minutes of struggling and one hell of a balancing act, Lane stood atop the electrical box with a hold on the small drain pipe located on that side. Bracing his foot on the two foot wall once again, he pushed himself high while pulling on the small pipe. Several more minutes and a whole lot of scratches later, Lane was able to hoist himself over the ledge and onto the second floor of the garage annex.

Making a quick scan of his immediate surroundings, Lane was relieved to find that no cameras were recording his efforts. He scouted the five floors of the garage, locating and avoiding cameras on each floor. The cameras monitored bridge ways, which connected the garage to the courts building at each floor and were, therefore, easily evaded. Finally on the final floor, Lane found what he was looking for, the reserved parking space of Judge Bill Rights. Satisfied that his guess proved correct, Lane searched the building for a place to hide until court was in session, and then he'd implement the next step of his plan. He found an unlocked maintenance room that was apparently used for storage.

Lane made himself some space behind a stack of fluorescent bulbs and, using the napsack he had with him as a headrest, he stretched out on the floor with his suppressed nine mm at the ready. Having set the alarm on his watch for ten a.m., he allowed himself to drift into a light slumber.

* * *

At precisely ten a.m., Lane's rest was disturbed by the irritating sound issuing from his wrist watch. Rising to a sitting position, he took a few minutes to re-orient himself with his surroundings and to clear the cobwebs from his head, before he turned the alarm off. Gathering his gear, Lane cautiously left the maintenance room and crept back to the reserved parking space of Judge Bill Rights.

Lane checked the license number on the Lincoln that occupied Rights space to be sure that this was the right one. Smiling to himself, he went to work. First, Lane located the fuel tank then he pulled the three quarter block of C-4 and activated the phone whose ring would ignite the explosives. Finally, he checked the battery's charge and attached the package to the Lincoln's fuel tank using the strong adhesive strips.

Lane gave a little tug against the powerful glue to satisfy himself that the package would remain in place should the vehicle experience any bumpy terrain. Again, he smiled as he crawled out from under the judges Lincoln, but the smile quickly disappeared. Standing just a few feet from Lane was a security guard who had been making his patrol on that floor. Luckily the guard hadn't spotted Lane, yet dumb luck would have it that guard stopped his patrol here at the rear of the judge's car. Quietly, Lane withdrew his suppressed weapon, braced himself in his prone position and took careful aim at the guard's head. Lane could only think of four words at that moment . . . Shit, Shit, Shit and Shit!

The guard casually pulled a pack of Marlboros from his pants pocket, withdrew a lighter from the other and lit one. Lane watching him closely as the guard took a long pull from the smoke, but held it in for what seemed to Lane as an excessively long time. When the guard finally blew out a large cloud of smoke and leaned on the trunk of Right's Lincoln, the area filled with the smell of marijuana. Four new words came immediately to Lane's mind, who was allergic to the illegal plant. Fuck, Fuck, Fuck and Fuck!

Lane took a deep breath to prevent inhaling any of the chemical that now surrounded him. One sneeze and he'd have to kill this guy, that meant more work and Lane desperately wanted to get away a.s.a.p. because he had to make a purchase before court let out.

Both men jumped and Lane nearly killed the guard when the radio on the young mans belt came to life.

"Hey Tommy! Tommy we've got a problem down here! I need your help." The static filled voice came over the air.

Tommy signed and grabbed up his radio, "Can't it wait, I just started my break!"

"Sorry, Tommy! There was a wreck out front and the boss wants one of us to direct traffic until the H.P.D. arrives."

Speaking to himself, Tommy mumbled some undecipherable curse, then into the radio he responded, "Alright Carl, I'm on my way. Out!"

Clipping the radio back to his belt, Tommy sighed, "Dammit!" Then he put away his marijuana cigarette and took off at a run.

Lane waited until he couldn't hear any more footfalls then took in several big gulps of air into his burning chest. Instantly, he began to sneeze and cough, his eyes burned and his vision blurred. "Fucking dope nearly got him killed! The stupid bastard!" He mumbled while gathering his gear together.

* * *

Lane kept a close eye on his watch, while he shopped for a cheap cell phone. Settling for a 'GO' phone and twenty-five dollars worth of minutes, he hurried back to the courthouse downtown.

Across from the courts building and the adjoining garage annex, Lane parked in a pay for space lot and waited for court to let out for lunch. He hoped that Rights would leave the building at that time and there was a good chance. Usually, only the more high profile trials resume after the lunch hour and Lane couldn't find any trials of that nature in Judge Rights' court listing.

Lane spotted Rights' Lincoln exiting the parking garage and quickly fell in behind him a few care lengths back. Following the judge out of downtown and onto I-10 Lane fingered the two phones he now possessed. The phone used for triggering the bomb was set next to him on the seat and with the 'GO' phone he'd bought earlier Lane entered the judge's cell phone number.

"This is Bill." The judge answered on the third ring.

"Hello Judge. If you don't do exactly as I say, your fancy new Lincoln will explode, leaving little pieces of your dead body all over the highway."

After a short pause Right asked, "What do you want? If you want money, I have . . ."

The judge was cut off by Lane's laughter.

After a brief pause the judge said "Ok, so it's not money, then what is it?"

Rights tried to remain calm, he wasn't even sure that his car would explode. After what happened to the former D. A. he wasn't taking any chances, although this certainly didn't seem like the m.o. of the guy who killed LeGross.

"What I want your honor is something you specialize in, Justice. All I want is a little justice," Lane said smugly.

"Who the hell are you? Why *me*?" Rights pleaded.

"All in time, Bill." Lane responded quickly. "First you need to know that if you try to exit the highway, you'll die. Just take it easy and keep heading west or the Lincoln will explode. Know that I can see you, so if you do anything that I don't like . . . well, I don't like repeating myself too much. Now, I have a couple of questions Bill. First, I want to know about Detective Von Eric, what type of cop is he."

Confused by the question, Rights answered, "He's a straight cop."

"Bill, I'm not asking about his sexual preferences. I want to know if he's dirty. Like you!" Lane's anger began to show in his tone.

"No!" Rights answered quickly in an attempt to ease Lane's anger, "No he couldn't be bought. We tried!"

Lane thought for a second, "And by we, you mean T.A.C. is that right.

Now Rights was surprised and wasn't sure how to answer. Finally, he admitted, "Yes, that's right."

"Well, who's the one to call off the dogs?" Lane asked flatly.

Rights didn't understand what he meant, "I'm not sure I understand what you're asking."

"Smarten up judge, or I'll kill you here and now!" Lane growled into the phone. "Who the fuck do I have to kill to keep T.A.C. from looking for me?"

Rights, grimacing at the blunt question, finally understood who he was talking with. He couldn't give J.T. away because that would probably come back to him hard! But then he didn't want to risk getting killed by the guy on the phone. Finally he answered, "I'm not sure. I go through channels or receive instructions via E-mail. I've never met any of them in person."

Lane slowed his truck, falling away from the judge's luxury car. "You're useless Bill", he stated while exiting I-10 onto Beltway eight. "You helped to send me, an innocent man, to the pen. For your crimes in abusing your office, I'm sending you to hell." Lane plugged the speed dial key on the other cell phone. "Good-bye bill. May the devil devour your soul!"

As soon as the words left Lane's lips, Big Time Bill Rights' new Lincoln exploded. The explosion shook the ground and rocked the nearby cars, sending some smashing into the concrete barriers that separated the east bound and west bound lanes while others were sent careening off the highway, jumping the curb into the grassy medians which separated the highway from the feeders.

Lane could see the rolling black smoke rise into the air as he topped the overpass which would carry him onto the belt way. "Go to hell, you bitch," he mumbled to himself.

Chapter Ten

* * *

"GOD DAMN YOU, Bryant!" Osbourne cursed to himself. Looking at the small monitor, which held the tracking device attached to Lane's truck then back to the wreckage that lay ahead, he knew Lane wouldn't attempt to expose Rights. There would be simply too much heat drawn by the death of the judge.

"Shit!" Osbourne cursed again as he plugged away at the digits on his cell phone.

Traffic slowed to a stop while he waited for someone to answer so he simply pulled to the shoulder, navigated his vehicle over the curb and drove through the small grassy median to the feeder road.

"Hello." Came a woman's voice over the phone.

"We'll have to move the operation forward. I'll be there sometime before midnight tonight."

"Dave . . . Ok, um, when were you thinking of having the alterations performed?"

Osbourne grimaced as the traffic once again came to a stop.

"First thing in the morning. I've some business to take care of then I'll be out to see you. Just be ready to go at day break." Osbourne ended the call then took the first road he came to, leaving the area.

* * *

Having been working in the kitchen preparing dinner for her and her husband, Beatrice took a small break from her house work to watch her favorite soap opera. Instead of her show, however, was a news break with live coverage from a circling helicopter. The view showed many emergency vehicles, lights flashing and traffic backed-up for miles.

A news personality was talking of an explosion that killed one person, who was unidentified at this time, and caused several wrecks which injured more than a few others.

"Oh, Dear Lord." Beatrice whispered under her breath.

The doorbell rang, drawing Beatrice from her reverence. She turned the large screen off then headed to answer the door. When she arrived she spied through the eyehole to see a well groomed and well dressed middle aged man holding an expensive looking black leather doctors bag.

The neighborhood which she lived in was and expensive gated community with its own armed security force and has never seen any problems such as home invasions, as long as she could remember, so Beatrice didn't think twice about opening the door.

"Yes?" She asked curiously.

"Beatrice Rights" The well groomed man asked.

"Yes."

I'm Detective Enis Von Eric with the Houston Police Department. May I come in?" Dave Osbourne smiled and flashed a phony badge he had made for just such an occasion.

"Why . . . yes, detective." Mrs. Rights answered worriedly, standing aside to allow Osbourne passage.

Osbourne accepted the invitation walking past the judge's wife then he stopped, allowing her time to shut the door and lead him further into the house. Once she took the lead, Osbourne reached into the bag he carried, withdrew a suppressed nine millimeter and fired two rounds into the woman's back. The woman pitched forward, landing face down, motionless. The former detective pulled on a pair of latex gloves he'd retrieved from his pocket and set out to complete his task.

Taking a quick inventory of the Rights' home, Osbourne hurried to the judges' office. He moved the heavy desk out of the way and rolled back the carpet. He then retrieved an electric drill and bits from his bag, plugged it up and went to work opening the safe that was hidden in the floor.

After a while the safe opened and Osbourne grabbed his prize along with two hundred thousand dollars. Not bothering to clean any of the mess he'd made, Osbourne left the house and the neighborhood following the direction of the small hand held monitor, which would lead him to Lane Bryant's truck.

* * *

Junior homicide Detective Enis Von Eric waited patiently in a lot designated for police to park their personal cars. Downtown Houston is full of one way streets, this street runs next to the Courts building and garage annex that services it. Anyone who parks at that annex, such as Judge Rights, would drive past this lot when leaving.

Traffic increased dramatically when court adjourned. Von Eric cranked his vehicle's engine and crept near to the exit looking carefully for Rights' white Lincoln. Soon he was awarded for his patience when Rights drove by in the slow flow of autos. Von Eric had to wait for a break in the traffic that he could squeeze into, before he could pick up the judges tail. While he was waiting to pull out of the lot, he spotted Lane's Chevy already in pursuit of Judge Rights and panic struck the heart of the detective. If he lost Lane the judge would be dead and there would be no evidence to convict the murderer. As Lane's truck got increasingly farther away, Von Eric's anxiety climbed and climbed until finally he just jumped his car out into the traffic, causing several small fender benders.

Not able to worry about what repercussions would rise from those people reporting his license plate number, Von Eric focused on catching up to Lane. He managed to stay behind the two all the way to the highway. Once on the highway, Von Eric took the chance to close in on Lane's truck to be sure he was the one driving the vehicle. He confirmed that it was Lane, noting that he was talking into a cell phone. Having satisfied his curiosity, Von Eric dropped a few cars away from him and maneuvered his car into the outside lane in case Lane decided to exit. That way if Lane looked to the rear, it wouldn't appear that he was being followed.

Just a short while later, as the three members of this unexpected convoy neared the Beltway 8, Lane veered toward the exit ramp. The Beltway rose over I-10 on Houston's west side so the feeder that connected I10's west bound lane had to rise to the overpass to connect to the north bound lanes of the Beltway. Noting that the judges Lincoln kept west bound Von Eric had to make a quick decision and chose to follow Lane instead. As the exit neared an explosion rocked the area and Von Eric gaped in unbelief at the wreckage that remained where Judge Rights' Lincoln had been only milliseconds earlier.

"Unbelievable." The detective whispered in awe. Then a moment later, "Brilliant . . . God damn you Bryant. That was brilliant."

The detective nearly rear ended the vehicle in front of him, who'd screeched to a halt near the rising exit ramp. Managing his own vehicle with practiced skill, Von Eric tapped his brakes and swung around the halted vehicle missing it by inches. The initial shock began to wear away and Von Eric's thoughts began calculating and working through the various scenarios, which might bring Lane to justice. All he had at this point was superstitions and allegations based on circumstantial evidence nothing that would hold up in court. He ultimately decided to follow Lane for awhile hoping something more concrete would turn up. However, if Lane attempted to leave the county he would have to make an arrest and that could cost him the conviction. Time will tell.

Von Eric, following Lane toward north Houston saw a massive storm rolling in from that direction. Even from this distance, he could distinguish the torrents of falling rain from the dreary dark mass which carried them. A few minutes of listening to a local radio station informed him that heavy thunder storms had developed and would be arriving that night.

Von Eric later found himself sitting in his car parked inconspicuously between two other vehicles at the far end of a nearly full lot where Lane rented a hotel room. He periodically switched from keeping and eye on Lane's truck to the lightning of the closing storm as he continued to consider his options.

The bottom line, he thought to himself, is I don't know how to proceed but I can't just let him go either. The best thing I can do, the detective continued in his thoughts, is wait and hope that something shows itself. Just as he finished his line of thinking, something did show itself in the form of the late Dave Osbourne.

* * *

Chapter Eleven

LANE WANTED TO get out of the area before the rain hit. Looking out from his hotel window, he knew that it was probably too late for that. Although rain hadn't actually started to fall, the night sky was being completely erased by the invading army of black masses firing their lightning bolts at the defenseless world below. Lightning blew up the sky, followed closely by the explosion of warring thunder. Dave Osbourne stood next to a Peterbuilt semi-truck watching when Lane returned to his Chevy with his travel bag in hand. Lane had exited the hotel at the rear, oblivious to the fact that anyone, especially Dave Osbourne, was watching him.

The Chevy sat parked next to a trash compacter in a corner of the lot closest to the hotel. The compacter was surrounded by wood fencing intended to protect the hotel's patrons from the unsightly machinery. A double gate offering access to the contraption inside stood open; its broken hinges defeated the purpose of the fence. A strong breeze, being pushed by the storm, carried the acrid odor of the compacter's contents to Lane's nostrils. Standing at the driver's door of his Chevy, Lane crinkled his nose at the unpleasant aroma as he slid the door key home to unlock it.

"Don't move Bryant, or I'll kill you where you stand." Lane, recognizing Osbourne's voice immediately, cursed himself for his stupidity.

"Drop your bag and place your hands on the roof of the truck, slowly." Lane followed the former detective's instructions allowing his forehead to come to rest against the window of the driver's door.

Shaking his head slowly, Lane said, "Never trust a cop!" and again cursed himself under his breath.

"That's right, Bryant," came Osbourne's response as he placed the muzzle of a gun at the base of Lane's skull, who again breathed another curse to himself.

"We had an arrangement, but you breached the contract . . ."

"Obviously, not before you!" Lane spat, cutting off the former detective.

Why are you here, Osbourne? I'd have never known you were still alive otherwise. You're taking a big risk exposing yourself."

"A necessary risk, I'm afraid," Osbourne's calm demeanor unsettled Lane. "I couldn't risk you accidentally discovering I wasn't dead. That might have proven disastrous for the new business I've just acquired from the late judge."

"You son of a bitch," Lane growled through clenched teeth. "You never wanted to expose the judge's activities! You just wanted me to get into that safe for you."

Lane's rising anger triggered an internal chaos, which began swirling and rolling. He heard himself shout above nearby rolling thunder, "I should've just shot your crooked ass!"

Osbourne laughed quietly, "You'll never be able to imagine my surprise when you didn't. What were you thinking? You actually believed I'd poison myself, didn't you? I'd already been planning my own death—everything was in place, now I'll have a new life, a new identity and a new occupation."

Osbourne paused a moment as fat drops of rain began to slowly fall then he continued, "I saw how you offed Rights. If I'd known you were so creative and resourceful, I probably would've made you a deal instead of sending you to the pen. But that's a moot point now, isn't it?"

Osbourne pressed the gun harder into Lane's skull, as he whispered into Lane's ear. "Don't—even—breathe, or I'll blow your head off!"

Lane didn't hear a word of Osbourne's threat. Voices in his head rose and fell in some sort of twisted and sadistic composition. Osbourne made a quick search of Lane's person, finding Lane's suppressed nine millimeters, the forty five and the trigger phone used to set off the bomb that killed Rights, all contained in Lane's napsack. Lane remained oblivious to his surroundings, but some inner conscious caused him to tighten his muscles in preparation to move quickly.

Lightning split the sky turning darkness into light and was instantly followed by a monsterous explosion. The sparse, fat drops of rain increased their descent then, as though in a coordinated attack with the previous bolt, a second struck in the very lot where Osbourne and Lane stood. The booming rapport that fell with the bolt shook the windows of the hotel and ordered the release of all the heaven's rain. In moments, the world around Lane was completely soaked in water yet Lane remained seemingly unaware.

Osbourne grabbed Lane's left hand and, twisting hard, bent it up behind his back. He then holstered his own gun and armed himself with one of Lane's nine millimeters. He raised the suppressed weapon to Lane's head ready to pull the trigger, when a familiar voice rang out above the tumult of the storm.

"Hold your fire, Dave!"

* * *

Von Eric was lost in contemplation when Lane exited the hotel but when Dave Osbourne crept out from the large red Peterbuilt rig he snapped. All of the suspicions he'd felt about the death of his former partner, suspicions he'd been forced to put on hold because of his present case, came back in a stunning flood.

"Damn." He whispered under his breath wondering what this new development could mean.

Was Dave working with Bryant? Or could it be that the supposedly late detective was in fear for his life and, therefore, opted to search Lane out. With his head spinning, Von Eric got out of his car and ran as quietly as possible to the large rig he'd seen Osbourne come from. He slowed to a crouched walk as he approached the rear of the rig. Looking around the corner, Von Eric saw Lane standing at his truck, both hands on the cab's roof and his head resting against the door. Standing behind Lane was Osbourne holding a gun against Lane's skull; he appeared to be having a conversation with Lane.

Von Eric crept around the rear of the Peterbuilt and along the side toward the cab's passenger door, remaining couched as he moved. He wanted desperately to hear what was being said so that he might have some indication of what was transpiring. Lightning struck as he rounded the rigs rear tires, causing him to dive on the ground and scrape his chin on the concrete.

"Shit," he whispered at length, as he got back to his feet drawing his department issued firearm.

Rain began to fall lazily around Von Eric as he reached the front of the rig. A breeze carried Osbourne's voice to Von Eric's ear in bits and pieces.

"I . . . offed Rights . . . made . . . deal . . ."

"It wasn't Lane at all." Von Eric said to himself. Von Eric watched Osbourne search Lane as he stood erect and stepped away from the rig, taking aim at the former and thought to be dead Detective Osbourne. Von Eric's vision was mangled by the bright flash of lightning that whitened the dark night and his nerves frayed with the following clap of thunder.

The lazy rain quickened its pace as Von Eric struggled to right his vision. Nearly as soon as his vision readjusted to the dark another radiant light flashed, turning the world white. As the thunder rolled away into silence the rain transformed into a giant waterfall, the noise of which hindered any chance from hearing any more of what was being said between the two he was spying on.

When Von Eric could see again in the night he noticed Osbourne, who now had Lane's arm locked behind his back, holster one pistol and draw another. One with a sort of extension that the detective thought he recognized as a suppressor. He watched Osbourne raise the weapon to Lane's head.

Von Eric shouted above the rain, "Hold your fire, Dave!"

* * *

Osbourne jerked, in shock, at the sound of his former partner's voice but he held his position, the suppressed pistol aimed at Lane's head. In Lane's mind, however, something clicked in a sound audible only to him then he clenched his right fist and grinded his teeth.

"Wait." Lane's inner voice instructed, drowning out the ruckus of rain and thunder. Acutely aware of his surroundings and of the gun aimed at his head, Lane remained calm with his muscles tight and ready to whip into action.

The din of the storm was so loud that Osbourne had to yell for Von Eric to hear him. "What are you doing here Enis? How'd you find me?"

"Actually I thought you were dead even though I still had some questions about it, I just haven't had the time to explore any of them. I was investigating Bryant and found that you had risen from the grave. Now put down the gun Dave."

Looking at Lane Osbourne asked, "Are you still so naïve to think that you can do some good in this world?" he took a quick glance toward Von Eric. "You still haven't learned *anything* I've tried to teach you."

"You've got nothing to teach Dave! I've finally got you. Put the gun down. Do it slow, do it *now*!"

Motionless, Lane listened intently to the exchange between Osbourne and Von Eric. He could feel Osbourne's eyes burning into the back of his skull and felt the tension in the former detective's grip on his wrist.

"Wait!" the tyrannical voice ordered Lane once again.

Osbourne turned to look at Von Eric through the pouring rain keeping the nine mm leveled at lane's head. Von Eric held a steady bead across the lot, aiming at Osbourne's chest.

It was a slight standoff in which Osbourne recognized his dilemma immediately. If he shot Lane then Von Eric would surely hit his mark. If he turned the gun on Von Eric, however, he'd never have the time to get a shot off before he got hit himself. Von Eric, for all his faults, was an excellent marksman but wouldn't risk hitting Bryant by firing first; it was a stand-off indeed.

A cataclysmic eruption of brilliant light and booming thunder exploded against the windshield of the Peterbuilt rig Von Eric stood next to. Von Eric jumped in shock of how close he'd come to being struck, if the large truck hadn't been there surely he would have been hit. The blast took him by surprise and when he jumped, he brought his gun toward the disturbance. A split second later he realized his mistake and began to correct himself but it was already too late. Before he could get his gun back to cover Osbourne the former detective had gotten a shot off.

The round from the suppressed nine caught Von Eric low in his throat rocking him back just a bit and burning like hellfire. His shot was blinded by his watery and blurred vision and he couldn't tell if he hit his mark. As soon as he fired, Von Eric felt an explosion high in his chest from Osbourne's second round.

* * *

Lane remained perfectly still and aware. He sensed the aim of the pistol pointed at his head shift away and heard the quiet *spith* of a round being discharged. The grip on his left wrist loosened but by then Lane was already in action, the tyrannical demand for vengeance echoed within.

Lane's vicious right elbow came around violently in a downward arch into the bridge of Osbourne's nose as Lane twisted from his captor's vice. The unexpected blow flashed white behind Osbourne's eyes just as he squeezed the trigger a second time. Instantly Osbourne felt the burn of hot lead as a bullet sank deep into his abdomen and he knew that Von Eric had shot him.

* * *

The force of the impact rocked Von Eric back a couple of stumbling steps. Suddenly he was drained of energy and needed to rest. He unintentionally dropped his gun, took another unstable step back then fell to his rump looking at the blood beginning to saturate his clothes.

The pour of the rain slowed to a steady fall which felt good to his ashen face as he looked to the sky. It took him a moment to understand that he was lying on his back and he was unable to move his limbs as his vision began to darken around him.

He tried to swallow but even that proved to be too much for him to accomplish. He could only lie on his back and wait, his mental functions slowly evading him. A sound brought him back from the edge of death, a familiar voice.

Von Eric forced his focus on Bryant who now stood over him. "You might have just saved my life detective." Lane's voice was as clear as an angel's herald.

* * *

Lane's elbow destroyed Osbourne's nose, lying it over flat. He followed the strike with a downward chop that sent the weapon Osbourne held sliding across the concrete. The gun skittered under a nearby car as Osbourne spun from the round Von Eric fired. Lane looked to Von Eric in time to see him drop his gun and fall to his rump.

Knowing that Osbourne had just been shot gave Lane's already high confidence a boost even though he knew that the former detective still had a gun. Lane spun back around in the opposite direction from his first attack, hammering his fist into Osbourne's wounded side and forcing a pain-filled grunt from him.

Osbourne half stumbled, half ran from his attacker while holding his wound with one hand and grasping for his holstered gun with the other. Lane was on Osbourne's heels and, smelling blood, slipped into a maniacal rage.

"Where are you goin', you fuck?!!" Lane growled, hammering a furious left into Osbourne's temple. Osbourne couldn't defend himself; the left hook came over his shoulder from behind and sent him stumbling to his right, around the front of Lane's truck. For a moment Osbourne forgot his gun, instinctively putting his hand to his head. Lane's fury escalated.

Following Osbourne around the front of the truck lane promised, "You're gonna die you crooked shit! I'm gonna make sure of it!" Spittle flew from Lane's lips as he swore his oath.

As he spoke, Lane took one step in pursuit of Osbourne and placed a solid forward kick into the man's lower back. Osbourne was sent careening forward several feet, landing face first onto the concrete sidewalk near the trash compacter.

Face scratched and bleeding, Osbourne struggled to climb to his hands and knees. Excruciating pain from his gunshot wound ran through his upper body like jolts of electricity causing him to sway left and right in the knelt position.

"You summoned my demon you piece of trash, now you'll reap its rage!" Saliva fell heavily from Lane's bared teeth like that of a rabid dog. Still on his hands and knees, Osbourne reached for his holstered sidearm but Lane anticipated the attempt. As Osbourne's fingers gripped the pistol Lane jumped high into the air and before the weapon could be fully drawn he was atop of Osbourne.

Landing feet first with all of his might onto Osbourne's back, Lane drove him back down to the sidewalk with a sickening crunch of bone. For a moment Lane thought he'd broken Osbourne's back but after unclipping the holster then tossing it with the gun aside he realized it wasn't his back that was broke.

The breath had been driven from Osbourne's lungs and as he gasped for air his mind tried to register the reason why his arm wouldn't respond to his command. He felt Lane unclip the holster from his waist but couldn't feel any part of his right arm beyond the mounting pain in his shoulder. Unconsciousness threatened to overtake him under the weight of his assailant.

A sense of weightlessness came over Osbourne as Lane hoisted him off the ground, "Time to take out the trash detective." Lane said smiling, knowing there was no fight left in the man. As he spoke, Lane half carried half shoved Osbourne, driving him face first into the metal side of the large blue trash compacter that serviced the hotel.

Osbourne slumped to the ground defeated but Lane wasn't finished with him yet. He grabbed a handful of Osbourne's matted hair, dragging him to his feet. Still holding Osbourne's hair, Lane smashed his head into the compacter again. Then again . . . and again, growling "Fuck you! Fuck you!" over and over, punctuating every syllable with every impact

Lane slowly calmed noticing for the first time that the downpour slowed to a drizzle, although lightning wasn't far away and its thunder still sounded lightly in the distance. He also noticed that Osbourne was unconscious in a bloodied heap at his feet. Lane looked at the downed man for a long moment then picked him up and unceremoniously dumped' him in the compactor.

Lane went in search of the napsack and the nine mm that had been knocked to the ground and he was curious to see if Von Eric had survived. The pistols were found easy enough because he'd known about where they fell. He clipped the holstered pistol to his waist, but kept the nine in hand as he approached the wounded detective.

Von Eric looked bad, but not critical although his breathing was shallow and he seemed to have a hard time focusing. Lane thought that shock would be the more dangerous of Von Eric's threats . . . He would survive.

"You might have just saved my life detective," Lane stated flatly. Von Eric forced his wild eye gaze toward Lane's voice.

"You look pretty banged up, Detective." Lane continued looking over Von Eric for any other injuries.

He took note of the detective's police radio, "Can I get you some help with that radio?" Lane asked pointing at the detective's radio.

Von Eric could only blink his response.

"Osbourne and LeGross both said you were a straight cop; a good cop." Lane knelt beside Von Eric as he spoke in a comforting voice.

"To be honest," Lane continued, "I never believed there was such a thing as a *good* cop"

Von Eric stared hard at Lane and with much struggling, he managed a very weak, "Help . . . m . . . me."

Lane nodded, "Alright, I'll help you." He then stood and fired two rounds into Von Eric's head.

"*Now* you're a good cop Enis!" Lane said aloud.

* * *

Osbourne returned from unconsciousness and slowly came to understand where he was. Blood oozed from the hole in his side and his left arm was useless. As the fog over his mind lifted and his thoughts cleared, the danger of his position shot panic through him. Osbourne scrambled as best he could to get to his knees, thinking that he was already facing the exit. To his shocking horror, Osbourne discovered that the exit was behind him at the same moment the machine came to life and began to close on him. He cried and whimpered helplessly, as he struggled to change position in the cramped space.

Osbourne had managed to twist his way around and was at the exit when he felt something grab his foot, but he jerked away before he was trapped. He looked up to see Lane at the exit with a satisfied smile spread across his face. The machine clamped on him again, but this time, Osbourne was unable to free himself of the monster's clutches.

"You're the last Osbourne. Justice has been served." Lane announced, but Osbourne was screaming in agony and couldn't hear.

The screams came to an abrupt halt when the machine grasped Osbourne at the lower part of his ribs. Lane thought he could hear the cracks and pops of the crunching bones and that caused his smile to broaden. He continued to watch as the former detective was slowly bit in half.

He watched Osbourne's eyes bulged out so much they looked as if they'd pop out. He watched as Osbourne's upper body twitched in spastic jolts, as though electricity was coursing through it. Lane continued to watch until the compactor reopened, allowing Osbourne's upper torso to slide back into the murderous contraption with a thick, wet 'splat'.

Lane removed his soaked tee shirt, wiped his prints from the machinery and pistol then placed Osbourne's print on the butt and trigger of the silenced 9mm, dropping it outside of the compactor in a place easy to find.

Discarding all of his remaining gear, including Osbourne's gun and the equipment Trigga gave him in his usual manner, Lane felt relieved to be leaving Houston. Hopefully for the last time!

Epilogue

LANE TOOK A couple of days to get home, so that the minor scuffs and bruises he'd endured would heal some. He timed his arrival so that he could already be home when Carol got in from work. He also took the time to stop and buy a large stuffed teddy bear that stood nearly five feet and a large missing you card, both of which he placed in the center of the living room.

He parked his truck at the far end of the apartments so that it couldn't be seen and walked back to his apartment. Sitting on his bed he used his lap top to log on to the various Houston news channels. His sense of satisfaction increased with every station he viewed.

Through the various stations, he discovered that the murders of Judge Bill Rights, District Attorney Keith LeGross and HPD Detective Enis Von Eric were all a conspired effort coordinated by former HPD Detective Dave Osbourne, who was believed to have committed suicide. The doctor, who signed the death certificate, is being investigated but no charges had been filed yet. Dave Osbourne was found dead in a trash compactor at a hotel in North Houston where Detective Von Eric was killed by four gunshot wounds inflicted by what appears to be the late Osbourne's weapon.

As the stories compiled Lane became increasingly intrigued. When the vehicle Osbourne had been using was discovered at the scene, documents were found connecting the late Judge Rights to Houston's most powerful gang. It is believed that the Texas Aryan Coalition or T.A.C. had organized a crime ring involving Rights, LeGross and Osbourne, as well as several other city officials. Joseph T. White, Mayor of Houston, has been implicated in several offenses and appears to be the highest ranking member of the white supremist organization. Mayor White refuses to comment at the time and has secluded himself at his Bellaire home in Fort Bend County. Charges have not yet been filed . . .

"Baby?" Carol's voice drifted in from the front room. Lane set his computer to the side and walked to the doorway to see his wife running her hand over the soft material of the giant bear.

"Don't you like it?" Lane asked.

Surprised Carol spun on her heels then ran the short distance to Lane's arms who lifted her off the ground like a little girl.

"I've missed you." Lane said kissing his wife and bringing her close in a big hug.

Returning Lane's show of affection, she responded the same, then looking straight at her husband she asked, "You're not going to leave again are you?"

He kissed her forehead, "No Baby. I don't need to go again," he smiled at the truth of what he was saying, "I've taken care of everything I could and the rest just fell into place . . . I'm done."

As the couple embraced again Lane's gaze was forced to a small mirror hanging on the wall on the far side of the living room. A menacing grin spread across Lane's reflected features followed by his demons vengeful snarl and Lane knew at that moment that whatever the future held, *he* was far from done.

DOWNTOWN CAMPUS LRC

JS Reynolds Community College
3 7219 00181370 1

HV 9468 .M33 A3 2011
McCord, F. Douglas.
Criminal Justice

DISCARDED